Ghost Tales of
the Moratoc

Ghost Tales of the Moratoc

by
Catherine T. Carter

John F. Blair, Publisher
Winston-Salem, North Carolina
TM

Printed on acid-free paper

Printed and Bound by Quebecor America Book Group
Designed by Debra L. Hampton

Library of Congress Cataloging-in Publication-Data

Carter, Catherine T., 1943–
Ghost tales of the Moratoc / by Catherine T. Carter.
p.   cm.
ISBN 0-89587-091-6 (hard : alk. paper)
1. Ghost stories, American.   2. Ghosts—North Carolina.
I. Title.
BF1472.U6C37   1992
133.1'09756'1—dc20
92–102

*To
Lawrence,
my husband and friend*

Contents

Preface

This volume of stories is the harvest reaped from growing up in a family of storytellers. The fair-weather Sunday afternoons of my youth were spent on the front porch listening to aunts and uncles tell the stories that had been passed down to them. When winter came and the nights grew frosty we moved indoors by the wood heater and the flickering light of the single oil lamp. We caught up on the week's news, and then the stories began. There was no television to intrude on our imaginations, no harsh ringing of a telephone. The only traffic was an occasional car or truck moving slowly, almost silently, on the bumpy dirt road in front of the house.

Listening to the "old" people tell eerie tales was magical and mesmerizing. The softness of their voices and the complete stillness that surrounded us, broken only by the sighing of the trees or our dog's baying at the moon, combined to draw us into a mood suspended from reality. My relatives asked their audience neither to believe nor disbelieve. Their stories were told for the sheer pleasure of the telling. But in their act of telling the stories they were passing to us our heritage, our family history and the history of our part of North Carolina.

I now tell some of those same ghost tales and legends myself. It seems that whenever I finish telling a story someone invariably asks whether I believe the story is factually true. My reply is always the same, that I take pleasure in the story but that I do not try to explain the unexplainable. That is exactly what I hope readers of this collection will do. I hope they will enjoy and take pleasure in the stories, no more and no less. There are things that are unexplainable, and perhaps they are best left that way.

There have been volumes of ghost stories and legends written about the Outer Banks and the mountains of North Carolina, but the northeastern part of the state—Washington, Martin, Bertie and Tyrrell counties—has been largely ignored. These are flatlands, where two-lane highways and dirt roads far outnumber sleek superhighways. This is farm and timber country. Tobacco, soybeans, corn, peanuts and cotton grow in fields bordered by acres and acres of hardwoods and pines. The four counties enjoy a common link with either the Roanoke River or Albemarle Sound.

It is a region of old families. Descendants of the pioneers still live in the area and own and farm their families' original land. There is a sense of pride in family history and family relationships. Fourth cousins once removed are still considered family, and family reunions are the biggest social events of the year. It is no wonder that stories abound in our corner of North Carolina— the Moratoc region.

The word *Moratoc* is an Algonquian name that translates as "nice river" or "good river." The name has been spelled a number of ways, but Moratoc is the oldest version. The river that is the lifeblood of the area was called the Moratoc until sometime in the eighteenth century, when it became known as the Roanoke. There was also an Indian village called Moratoc on the bank of the river, according to a map by John White, the sixteenth-century colonial governor. The village was located on a high sandhill near the present site of the town of Plymouth.

The first recorded visit of white men to the Moratoc region was in 1585, when Ralph Lane led an expedition into the vast, unexplored territory of dense forests. He had been appointed governor of the Virginia territory by the queen of England, and he was eager to make a good impression on his sovereign.

Lane was supposed to organize an English settlement on Roanoke Island, but he was more interested in discovering precious metals. His inspiration was the tales he and his men had heard the Indians on the island telling about the shiny, bright metals to be found in abundance along the inland rivers.

Those tales were fabrications. Who knows why the Indians should have invented such stories? Perhaps they did it for sheer amusement, or more likely to lure Lane and his band of Englishmen out of their territory. The Englishmen had worn their welcome thin, thanks to the many demands they made upon the Indians. The simple fact is that the ruse worked, and that Ralph Lane and his colonists went treasure hunting.

They visited territories on the north side of Albemarle Sound first, taking an Indian named Skyco, the son of Chief Menatonon, as a hostage. Then they crossed the sound and set their course for the Moratoc River.

Along the banks of the river lived the Moratoc Indians, believed to have been of Algonquian descent. Lane and his men had heard many strange tales about the river. The Indians said that it gushed forth from a huge rock that stood near the ocean, and that during storms the ocean waves beat into the rock and turned the river salty. But the story that most interested the white men concerned the copper and gold that were reportedly available for the taking.

Lane and his band of forty men traveled up the river in search of their fortune. Nowhere along the journey did the Moratocs come out to greet them. The adventurers had counted on getting corn and other food from the Indians to replenish their dwindling supplies. After they had journeyed more than a hundred miles upstream their food was gone and they still had found no evidence of the precious metals they sought. They returned disillusioned, weary and hungry to Roanoke Island. The first venture of Europeans into the area was thus a failure, and the Moratoc Indians were left in peace and saw no more white men until much later.

The British considered the northeastern part of North Carolina a good location for settlement and development because of its proximity to sounds and rivers. Shipping vessels could navigate the local rivers and provide ready transportation for the area's chief exports—lumber and farm produce. Small towns were subsequently founded along the banks of the waterways: Plymouth, Jamesville and Williamston on the Roanoke River; Windsor on the Cashie River; Edenton and Mackeys Ferry on Albemarle Sound; Columbia by the Scuppernong River. All of those communities are still alive and well today. Though small in size the towns have maintained their distinct characteristics over the course of their two hundred–plus years of existence.

That is the early history of the Moratoc region. Other bits and pieces of local history may be gleaned from the tales that follow. Many stories have undoubtedly been lost over the years. This collection was written in the hope of preserving some of the heritage of the region.

Many of the tales related here were told by friends and relatives who have long since passed away. Others were shared by people who are still very much alive. In my years as a librarian I have told many regional legends and ghost stories. Several stories included in this volume were favorites of my listeners. It is my hope that some of them will become your favorites, too.

Acknowledgments

My mother taught me that no individual ever achieves anything without the help of others. Many people gave me encouragement and advice and shared their stories with me when I was working on this book. I owe a special thank-you to them: Bea Tetterton, my aunt, who always believed that I would write this book; Brenda Bullock, my cousin, whose encouragement never waned; Gail White, my dear friend, who is always optimistic; Shirleyan Beacham-Phelps, a friend and writer, who listened to all my woes; Gail Roberson, another friend and writer, who encouraged me and shared her stories with me; Bob and Calla Tetterton, my parents, who taught me to love reading; and, finally, Sissie and Uncle Guy, who were the greatest of story-tellers, and who passed their love of stories on to me.

Ghost Tales of
the Moratoc

1 | *The Oyster Shells*

arming was the chief livelihood of most of the population in rural Washington County in the late 1800s. Few farms were prosperous, but somehow families managed to scratch out a living of sorts.

Miss Rosie and her boy, Sonny, tended one such "hand-to-mouth" patch of ground. They were tenant farmers, and theirs was a hard lot. Actually Miss Rosie's was a hard lot, for Sonny was about as trifling and good-for-nothing as a human can be. Local opinion was that he wasn't worth the powder and shot it would have taken to blow him up. But Miss Rosie loved him because he was her only boy.

Neighbors gossiped of seeing Miss Rosie plowing in the scalding July sun while Sonny rested in the shade of the porch. One neighbor told how she had heard Sonny call out to Miss Rosie to come and dip him a gourd of water from the well while he was stretched out on the porch resting. Miss Rosie informed her neighbors that Sonny had a delicate heart and that it was against him to do any hard work.

When Saturday night came Sonny headed for town, delicate heart or not. It was usually in the wee hours of Sunday morning when he came staggering up the lane to the house. Occasionally he would pass out in the ditch and just spend the night there.

The years rolled by and Miss Rosie grew old and feeble, but she still did all of the man's work on the little farm. Sonny grew robust and a little short of breath in his middle years. Everyone agreed he was totally worthless. To add to his abundant shortcomings he developed a nasty disposition. Neighbors talked of seeing bruises on Miss Rosie's face and arms. It was general gossip that Sonny frequently vented his foul moods on his old mother. Neither did his weekend habits change for the better, for every Saturday night found him carousing and drinking in town, and many a Sunday morning dawned to find him passed out in the ditch. But his delicate heart kept right on ticking.

Then a flu epidemic struck Washington County. Miss Rosie fell mortally ill. One Saturday afternoon a deacon from her church brought a bushel of fresh oysters for her. Oysters had long been her favorite food, and the deacon hoped they would perk her up a bit. Miss Rosie was mighty glad to get those oysters, and she begged Sonny to steam a few of them and bring them to her.

Sonny built a fire at the edge of the yard and commenced steaming the bushel of oysters. Every time he shucked some he threw the shells in a pile under Miss Rosie's bedroom window. From her bed she could smell the aroma of the freshly steamed oysters, and her mouth watered for a taste of them.

The afternoon was cloudy, with barely a sliver of sun in the steel-gray sky. It was a day to match Sonny's disposition, for he was in one of his black moods. The harder Miss Rosie begged for the oysters the more determined he was to eat every last one of them. When he had eaten all he could hold he threw the remaining oysters in the ditch. Then he sauntered into his mother's bedroom, still wiping the juice from his lips, and declared, "Them oysters sure were fittin', Maw!" Then he threw his head back and laughed his wicked laugh. Tears filled Miss Rosie's eyes, and her old heart nearly split open with its burden of sadness.

She knew that her time on earth was short, and she pleaded with Sonny not to go to town that night. But instead of heeding his dying mother's wishes Sonny slicked himself up and set off for the bright lights. The last thing Miss Rosie ever heard was his shrill, off-key whistle as he headed down the lane.

It was the early-morning hours before Sonny came back up the lane. He saw through his bleary, bloodshot eyes that lamps were lit all over the little house. He could just make out the shapes of several men who were gathered on the front porch. Sonny muttered and swore under his breath, staggering up the lane until some of the men grabbed him and pulled him up the porch steps.

A thick, ominous silence lay over the crowd assembled on the porch. Out of the group stepped one man dressed all in black. When he began to speak it was in a hushed and almost sinister tone. "Sonny," he said, "while you were in town carousing and drinking tonight your poor old mother died."

At this Sonny began to sway back and forth, sobbing and weeping and asking over and over, "What will become of me? Oh Lordy, what will become of me?"

"You cold-hearted scoundrel!" the man in black growled. "Not one of us is surprised that your only thought would be for yourself and not for your dear old mother. Her dying thoughts were for you, and with her last breath she left a message for you."

Sonny begged to hear his mother's last words, and finally the man told him. "It was just this: 'Tell Sonny I'll see him soon, very soon.'"

As they went inside the little house the neighbors pondered and whispered over Miss Rosie's last words, and some wondered aloud if perhaps her spirit might still be lingering nearby. In the meantime Sonny was kicking up a ruckus and hollering that he wanted to see his dear, dead mother. Some of the women had washed Miss Rosie and laid her out in her best black dress in the bedroom where she died, and it was there that Sonny was finally taken.

A single kerosene lamp cast a soft, unearthly light on the walls and their peeling wallpaper. The ragged curtains stirred ever so slightly, moved by an unseen breath of wind. Friends and neighbors filled the tiny room while Sonny slowly made his way to the bed. An eerie silence filled the air as he touched his mother's cold hand. Then from under the bedroom window came a clattering sound like that of a thousand tin cups being rattled together. All eyes were on the window as the noise become louder and shriller. A perfect likeness of Miss Rosie suddenly appeared above the pile of oyster shells, and in her clear, sweet voice she called out Sonny's name three times. The room was charged with the silence of stark terror as the image hovered and then faded away and the oyster shells were still once more.

For a few moments those gathered in the room were too stunned to comprehend what had taken place. They knew what they had seen, and yet they were afraid to acknowledge the presence of a ghost. When they again turned their attention to Sonny he was lying on the floor beside his mother's bed, one hand clutching his chest and the other firmly grasped in the deathly cold hand of Miss Rosie.

All attempts to revive him were unsuccessful. Sonny's delicate heart had at last failed him. Miss Rosie had made good her dying promise, for she indeed saw her son again very soon.

The little community was deeply saddened by Miss

Rosie's passing, but there was an unspoken sense of relief that Sonny would no longer be among them. The following day Sonny and Miss Rosie were buried side by side in the community's cemetery. A plain wooden marker was placed at the head of each grave.

But the story did not end there, for a few nights later a man walking by the cemetery saw a glow coming from Miss Rosie's grave. When he reached the grave he saw that it was entirely covered in oyster shells, all sparkling and glittering in the dark. No one ever discovered how the shells got there, but there they remained for years and years until time and the elements finally reduced them to the few chips that may be found today.

2 | *The Witch Hag of the Roanoke*

 n ghost lore and folk tales there are certain stories similar in makeup that are told and retold in different sections of a state or region. The settings and parts of the story may vary according to the storyteller and the region, but the versions are basically alike, and each region claims the story as its own. This genre of ghost lore is known as the traveling tale.

The Spearfinger story may well qualify as a traveling tale. Spearfinger, the wicked witch woman, is known in the North Carolina mountains as well as on the coastal plain. Some people believe that the same old hag once terrorized North Carolinians all the way from the mountains to the sea.

The common element among the different versions of the Spearfinger story is an evil woman who can change herself into any form she wishes, including that of a fleet-footed panther. What follows is the version of the story that is told in the northeastern section of North Carolina.

The Roanoke River, formerly called the Moratoc, has been home and refuge to man and beast for many centuries. The long and winding river is a mighty and a moody body of water. It stretches nearly four hundred miles from the hills of western Virginia to the lowlands of North Carolina, completing its rambling journey as it flows into Albemarle Sound.

In the 1800s the waters of the Roanoke were busy with the commerce of the small communities lying along its shores. Plymouth, Jamesville and Williamston were close enough to the mouth of the river to allow fairly large sailing vessels to navigate to their docks. But when the current was running strong it was a dangerous river even for the most experienced of sailors.

Abundant wildlife lives on the thickly wooded banks of the Roanoke. It is rich land that was formed millions of years ago when the sea retreated and left a soil of fine sand mixed with clay. The Algonquian tribes that once lived along the river were plentifully supplied with bear, deer, raccoon, wild turkey, squirrel, rabbit and many kinds of birds. From the river they took all the fish they could eat, and from the forest they took mosses, lichens and the bark of trees for a multitude of everyday uses. When white settlers came to the Roanoke they, too, reaped the harvest of the mighty waters and the woods.

But not everything that came from the forest was good. For nearly two hundred years something haunted the banks of the Roanoke, a mean and evil witch that could at will transform her bent and twisted body into anything she chose, be it man or beast. She lived in an underground cave deep in the piney woods and was an unseen witness to the daily hunting expeditions of the Indian tribes and the white settlers.

The Indians lived in terror of the witch woman. They gave her the name of Old Spearfinger, for in place of the index finger on her left hand was a razor-sharp steel blade that she used to slit the throats of her victims and cut the livers out of little children. Indian mothers learned never to send their children into the forest alone, for chances were good that they would not return. Some of the Indian children wore small bags of herbs tied around their necks, herbs that were blended by their medicine man to ward off witches.

Old Spearfinger was known to stalk the woods and villages on nights of the sickle moon. With just enough light for her to see, but not be seen, the nights of the sickle moon were the most opportune times for her to terrorize and maim and kill along the banks of the river. Indians and white men alike grew to dread those special times of the month. In the mornings, after a night of the old hag's rampaging, it was not unusual to find a full-grown deer ripped apart along the riverbank, its liver sliced out. That was a sure sign that Old Spearfinger had been on the prowl.

Old Spearfinger was exceedingly clever at changing herself into any form she chose. Most of all she liked to disguise herself as an old granny woman, for all appearances sweet, harmless and gentle. It was in the guise of the granny lady that she lured many innocent children to their doom.

Occasionally someone who was attacked by the vicious old witch would outsmart her and live to tell a chilling tale of near-death and escape. One such tale was told by a Martin County man.

The man was returning home from a church meeting one night. He wasn't paying much attention to the road as he galloped along, for his horse knew the way home. He was instead pondering some disagreeable business that had taken place at church. Suddenly his horse came to such an abrupt stop that he was almost thrown off. The man was peeved with the horse for its peculiar behavior, so he did not notice anything out of the ordinary at first. But then he began to feel as though he and his mount were surrounded by a circle of frigid air. He began to shake, even though it was a warm summer night. The horse, too, was trembling from the cold.

It was a night of the sickle moon, so only a small amount of light illuminated the road. As the man peered into the murky darkness he sensed, rather than saw, a bent and hunched-over figure standing in the middle of the road only a few yards ahead of his horse. The horse began to whinny, and with its head down and nostrils flared it started to paw the ground. The man dismounted and attempted to stroke the horse's head, thinking he could calm the animal. But the terrified horse broke away and headed back toward the church at a hard gallop.

The figure in the road moved closer. The man stood perfectly still, waiting to see who or what had so frightened his mount. "Good evening, kind sir," a gentle voice said. "I fear that I have given your horse a fright." Then the voice broke into a horrid, piercing laugh. The man backed away from the sound just as a tenuous streak of pale moonlight filtered across the figure's face. He saw that it was a very old and wrinkled woman. Her face was mostly concealed by a hood, but he felt a wicked gleam in her eyes.

Trying to control his fright he called out to her, "I say, old woman, what are you doing out on the road this time of night, and alone at that? You should be by your fire with your knitting and your pipe."

Again the high-pitched laugh came from beneath the hood of the old hag. "What am I doing? Scaring the horse out from under a fool like you!" Then she added in a scathing tone, "Churchgoer you were, but churchgoer you'll be no more after tonight!" All the while she kept moving closer and closer, and when she was just a few feet away the man could smell her foul breath. He kept backing away slowly but deliberately toward a nearby ditch.

As his eyes grew accustomed to looking at the woman he noticed that she had a basket on her right arm. Stalling for time he asked, "What have you got in that basket, old woman? Something for me, perhaps?"

"Not *for* you, my plump churchgoer. *From* you. I'll have your fat, juicy liver in my basket tonight." With that she lunged at him, and he saw the gleam of a razor-sharp steel blade as he jumped across the ditch just in time. She lost her balance and fell face down in the shallow ditch. The man ran as he had not run since he was a child. He ran as if he were pursued by a band of demons. He knew that his encounter had been with Old Spearfinger and that quite possibly he had not seen the last of her that night.

Indeed he had not, for as he took a shortcut through the woods he could hear a thudding sound in the distance behind him, a noise like that of a heavy animal at full speed. It drew rapidly nearer, and he turned his head just enough to see that he was being pursued by the largest panther he had ever encountered. The animal's eyes were blazing as red as hot coals and its ivory teeth were bared. It let go a scream that pierced the night and chilled the man to the depths of his soul.

He knew that he could not beat the big cat in a race,

so he desperately tried to recall any measure he had ever heard of that would repel a witch. The panther was so close that he could smell the stench from its skin and feel the heat of its body. With his breath coming in gasps and his legs buckling beneath him he reached in the pocket of his coat and grasped his black leather prayer book, and without considering the consequences he came to a dead stop in the path. Then, holding the prayer book with the gleaming gold cross on its cover high over his head, he turned to face the oncoming witch cat. "In the name of the Father, Son and Holy Ghost I command you to stop!" he shouted.

The animal was by then no more than ten feet from him. As the words came from his lips the huge panther turned into a ball of fire and disappeared completely, as though it had never been. The man continued on foot to his home, unmolested but much shaken by the events of the night. He was glad to be alive.

Not all encounters with Old Spearfinger ended so well, for most of her victims did not live to tell their tales of horror. People in the Martin County communities of Williamston and Jamesville often related hair-raising tales of the old witch and her evil doings. Legend has it that it was in Martin County that she met her doom.

It was a few years after the Civil War when the old witch went on a real rampage. Little had been seen or heard of her during the war. People hoped she had died or changed her territory, but that was not the case. Some very strange things began to happen. A farmer found his best milk cow lying in a pool of blood with her throat slit. And an old woman everyone called Cousin Sallie went out to her henhouse one morning only to discover her prize White Leghorn hens split open, with their livers removed.

First one and then another person reported seeing a very old lady with a hood pulled over her head carrying a basket on her right arm. The good citizens began to fear that Old Spearfinger had returned. There was talk that an enormous black cat was roaming the banks of the river, a cat that killed animals ruthlessly and then ate only their livers. One point agreed upon by everyone who saw either the old woman or the cat was that the creature had a razor-sharp blade on its left hand or forepaw. That weapon could not be concealed no matter how cleverly Old Spearfinger disguised herself.

Evil can be tolerated for only so long before disgust overcomes fear and the perpetrator has to be destroyed. That time had come for Old Spearfinger. The men of the community got together to plot the demise of the cruel witch who had plagued their lives for so many years.

It was a known fact that the old crone loved liver so much that she would have existed totally on that delicacy had it been possible. Of course she had her preferences, but she would eat any kind of liver as long as it was fresh and juicy. So it was decided that liver would be the bait to catch the wicked fiend.

It was All Hallows Eve when the men set up a table in a local graveyard. In the center of the table was a big, fresh hog's liver. The men concealed themselves in the nearby woods and waited and watched in uneasy silence. On the stroke of midnight a shadow crossed over the moon and a great wind blew up. Then suddenly an unearthly quiet settled over the graveyard, and as the men watched they saw Old Spearfinger at the table eating her fill of liver.

As stealthily as they could the men crept up behind her. She was caught off guard in her greed, and while four strong men held her down she was bound with a rope woven of white horsehair and a thread of silver, for a witch cannot break through a band of silver. The men hung on even though she kicked and screamed and yelled curses. Old Spearfinger was loaded onto a wagon drawn by a white horse. Her screams pierced the cold night air and struck terror into the hearts and souls of all who heard them. The frightened horse pulled its ghastly load until they reached an enormous old oak tree between Jamesville and Williamston.

The Hanging Oak was a giant among forest trees, a specimen so large that it was said three men could not encircle it with their arms. Its branches were so formidable that each in its own right would have made an admirable body for another tree. It is no wonder that such a noble and majestic tree was chosen for the auspicious deed of that night. Soon after the wagon came to a halt Old Spearfinger was hanged by the silver-laced rope until she was dead.

The news spread rapidly along the river, and the next day was one of rejoicing for all who had lived in the shadow of the evil witch for so many years.

The Hanging Oak is no longer standing. Even its stump is decayed and gone. There are some people who say that Old Spearfinger didn't truly die that night, that she still roams the banks of the Roanoke looking for her favorite feast, liver. But there are others who will tell you that on moonlit nights you can ride by the place where the mighty oak once stood and hear Old Spearfinger screaming as she did on the night she was hanged. They say the sound will put a chill in your heart.

3 | *The Restless Skull*

here are many superstitions associated with graveyards and the dead. It is not unusual for a person's remains to be moved from one cemetery to another, but the act is still performed with a certain degree of trepidation. There are many cultures in which it is taboo to disturb the final resting place of the dead, no matter how long they have been deceased. If you insist on defiling a grave then you had better be prepared to pay the penalty.

Bertie County lies between the Roanoke and Chowan rivers, with its southeastern point jutting into Albemarle Sound. Its land is fertile. From its earliest days Bertie County has been farm country, its economy based mainly upon its natural resources. Windsor, the county seat, is surrounded by farmland. Just a few miles south of that picturesque little town is the farm from which this story comes.

It seems that the farmer who owned the tract just south of Windsor had been planning to have a pond dug in his cow pasture for quite some time. On a couple of occasions he had made up his mind to do it and even set aside money to pay for the job, but he just hadn't gotten around to carrying out his plan. But the day finally arrived when the pond was dug at last. The farmer was busy with other work, and it was almost sunset before he climbed into his pickup truck and navigated the rutted lane to have his first look at the long-awaited pond.

The cows had already beaten him to it. They were gathered at one end of the pond, not bold enough to drink but so curious about the addition to their pasture that they had to inspect it at close range. The water was muddy from the recent digging, and the dirt around the edge of the pond was soft. By the time the farmer walked completely around the perimeter his boots were heavy with mud. He looked around for something to knock the mud off his boots and saw an object protruding a couple of inches through the damp soil. He bent over to retrieve it and grasped it with one hand, but the object was so cold and moist that his hand slipped off. Without straightening he clasped it with both hands and pulled with all his strength until he dislodged it from its resting place.

Even though the object was covered in mud it was clear to the astonished farmer that it was something quite out of the ordinary. After shaking the dirt off his boots as best he could he strode over to a hand pump near the edge of the pasture. The evening light was fading as the sun disappeared behind the big oak trees at the edge of the field, but as the water cleansed the object in his hands it became apparent that he was holding a perfectly preserved human skull.

The farmer kept pumping water over the glistening white object, awed and mesmerized by the porcelain quality of the piece of humanity he was holding. When it was as clean as plain water could make it he finally quit pumping. He used his handkerchief to dry the skull while he pondered what to do with it. Common sense and an even stronger feeling he could not name told him to put the skull back in the ground and cover it up, told him to walk away and forget about it. But he couldn't. He wanted the skull too much.

In the meantime darkness had crept up on him and he was still holding the skull in his hand. The farmer made his decision. He walked to his truck clutching his treasure to his chest, much like a child with a coveted toy. There was very little doubt in his mind that it was an Indian skull he had unearthed, for he had previously found arrowheads and other relics in that same piece of ground. It suddenly came to him that he had dug a pond right in the middle of an Indian burial ground, but at that moment he was too elated with his find to worry about the consequences.

His contentment was short-lived. When he got home he placed the gleaming head on the mantelpiece in his living room. After a hastily prepared supper he settled in with his newspaper, but he found that he couldn't concentrate on the lines of print. It seemed that the skull was willing his eyes to look at it. The farmer got up from his chair and moved to the sofa and proceeded to try to read again, but the same thing happened. Some unknown force was pulling his eyes from the paper to the mantel, and the skull was staring back at him through those awful, hollow sockets. The effect was more frightening than if the eyes had still been there.

The farmer was tired from a hard day's work and unnerved by the evening's events, so he decided to go to bed. He made his usual check around the house, shutting windows and locking doors, and when everything was secure he went to bed. But not before he had one last look at the skull.

It was the sound of the wind that woke him at three o'clock in the morning. He lay perfectly still as he watched the heavy damask curtains at his bedroom window billowing under the force of the blow. Yet the window remained tightly closed and securely locked! Soon afterwards a strange odor of herbs and wood smoke began to assail his nose. The farmer discovered that when he sat upright in bed the wind grew calm and the odor disappeared.

Some force he could not describe pulled him from his bedroom and down the hall and into the living room, where the skull was just as he had left it on the mantel. So weary was he that he wanted nothing more than to stop and rest in his chair, but something kept drawing him forward until he was at the front door.

The farmer opened the door and stepped out onto the porch, which was bathed in the light of the moon. There, standing in the yard just a few feet away, was an Indian brave. He wore a deerskin loincloth, and his long black hair stirred gently in the breeze. His face was serene and peaceful as he raised one hand in greeting.

How long they stood like that, gazing into each other's eyes, cannot be measured by the clocks of mortals. Neither spoke a word, but there passed between them an understanding beyond the bounds of spoken language. The farmer understood what the Indian brave wanted of him, and he nodded his head in assent and raised his hand to seal the commitment. The brave bowed his head in farewell as he silently slipped away into the dense forest.

Daybreak was still a few hours away. The farmer was anxious for it to arrive so he could fulfill his unspoken vow to the Indian. He went back inside the house and retrieved the skull from its resting place on the mantel. For the remainder of the night he sat quietly holding the skull and thinking.

He got up and dressed when the pink glow of the morning sun began to trickle through the pine trees. With the skull securely under one arm and a shovel under the other he went out to his truck, then drove slowly down the rutted dirt lane to the cow pasture and the freshly dug pond. The farmer turned over the earth at the place where he had found his treasure the day before, and then he replaced the skull and gently patted the moist, fresh dirt over it.

At the edge of the woods a tall figure dressed in a deerskin loincloth watched and raised his hand in a final salute before he disappeared for the last time.

4 | *A Mother's Love*

hosts, like the living beings they once were, come in two varieties, good and bad. It seems that the bad ones just keep coming around and being worrisome, which is probably what they did when they were alive. But a good ghost or spirit, or whatever it pleases us to call it, shows up for a very specific reason.

Most ghost stories are handed down from one generation to the next. It is a singular occasion when an individual admits that he or she has seen a ghost, then goes on to relate the story in faithful detail. This is the story of one of those singular occasions.

Williamston in the 1940s was typical of many small Southern towns. It was surrounded by abundant farmland, so it did a slow and leisurely business during the week. Saturday was the big day in town. Farmers and their families came in from the country to spend the day and spend their money. People visited on the streets. They ate hamburgers and barbecue at the cafes and took in the moving-picture show. A week's worth of excitement was bundled into a single day or even an afternoon. By dark the farm families were packing up and heading back home to the ever-present evening chores.

It was after dark that another side of Saturday appeared. That was when the juke joints opened and the night's entertainment began. For many citizens it was a harmless diversion in an otherwise dull week. But for those who were easily lured down the path of destruction it was a night of drinking and carousing that did not end until dawn. A week's wages could be spent in a single evening. Many a child suffered for the sake of its parents' weakness.

Such was the background of this story. The lady who shared it lived in a less-than-prosperous Williamston neighborhood. At the time the story took place she was a young teenager—young perhaps in years, but not in the ways of the world. She was already at that tender age both mother and father to her younger brothers, providing for their food and shelter with wages she earned by working at a nearby peanut mill. Occasionally she would be visited by her mother, but only when the errant mother wanted to borrow money for her Saturday-night carousing, after which she would disappear, not to be seen again for months.

The young girl was both respected and pitied by her neighbors, and although their finances were only a little better than hers they helped her whenever they could. The houses in that neighborhood, uniformly ramshackle and vermin-infested, were built side by side with dirt paths between them. Next door to the young girl was a neighbor woman who was especially kind. It was to this older woman that the young girl turned for the maternal advice and wisdom that her own mother denied her.

The neighbor woman had several children, and it just so happened that the oldest of them caught small-pox. The disease soon spread through the whole family. The mother nursed her children night and day for weeks, calling forth every old-time remedy she had ever learned in an effort to save her children from the ravages of the foul pestilence. Slowly and one by one the ailing children began to recover, but fate had not decreed that the impoverished little family should escape unscathed. Just as the older children were getting better their mother came down with the dread disease. The baby was still infected with the virus, too, and as the undernourished and exhausted woman tried to care for the infant she grew weaker and sicker.

Her young neighbor came daily and brought food and a homemade salve, which was applied to the baby's miserable sores. No doctor was called, for there was no money. Home remedies had to suffice.

As the days wore on the pox took its toll on the older woman. Her skin erupted in sores, and she burned with a high fever as she tossed from side to side in her bed. She knew that she was dying, yet her concerns and fears were not for herself, but for her desperately ill baby.

It was late one afternoon when she called her children to her bedside, and her tearful little family gathered around as she bade each one of them good-bye. But she made her final request to her young neighbor. "My greatest wish is for my baby boy to live," she said. "My time is short. Promise me you'll do all you can to save him. It means so much to me to know I'm leaving him with one who will love him and care for him. Please tell me you will."

With tears trickling down her cheeks the girl gave her solemn promise to do all that she could, but in her heart she did not believe she could save the critically ill little boy.

All through the seemingly endless night the girl tended mother and child, bathing their fevered bodies and giving whatever comfort she could. When morning finally came it brought with it sadness, for her neighbor and friend died just as the sun began to light up the sky.

The girl took the baby to her own home and sat by his side day and night, but to no avail. The little boy burned with fever, and no remedy that she tried brought his temperature down. The days and nights without rest, along with the many responsibilities she faced in raising her own family without the help of a parent, finally took their toll upon the girl. She fell asleep in a chair beside the baby's bed. Her sleep was one of sheer exhaustion.

She had no idea how long she had been at rest when she was suddenly wide awake. For a moment she could not believe what she saw, for bending over the sick baby was his dead mother. The girl was so mesmerized that she was unable to speak. She watched as the woman removed the cold towels that had been wrapped around the baby in an effort to break the fever. The woman then applied a greasy ointment to the infant's sores and put on fresh wet towels. Only once did the mother look away from her baby, and then she smiled and said, "It'll be all right. I've come back, just for a while."

The young girl had no recollection of going back to sleep, but when she awoke it was morning. The baby was lying peacefully in his crib, and when she felt his brow it was cool and there was no trace of fever. The sores on his little body were almost dry, and for the first time in days he was able to eat.

She was just at the point of believing that she had dreamed the events of the previous night when she walked around the side of the crib and found a pile of wet towels on the floor. Beside the towels was a small jar of ointment. It was then that she knew for certain that her old friend and neighbor had indeed come back and saved her baby's life.

There are some mothers who drink and carouse and leave their teenage daughters in charge of their families, but they are very much the exception. It has been said that a mother's love knows no bounds. That piece of wisdom has been proven true time and time again.

5 | *The Phantom of the Forest*

Many tales of the supernatural have been handed down by the great old storytellers of eastern North Carolina. A surprising number of those tales originated in the earliest days of the region, when hunting and trapping and fishing were skills that were absolutely necessary for feeding families. After a long day's hunt it was the custom for men to dress out their kill, then build a campfire and cook their meal. When they were relaxed by the food and the warmth of the fire they would tell stories of ghosts and phantoms and unexplained creatures that stalked the woods.

Not all of the tales involved evil spirits. One local favorite was the story of the Phantom of the Forest. The Phantom was a devoted friend of white men but a determined foe of all Indians. It was rumored that the Moratoc Indians had murdered his wife and baby and that he had declared his unceasing revenge from that day forward.

The Moratocs lived and hunted along the Roanoke River. The Roanoke was and is a beguiling river. Its waters can lie smooth and seemingly still, while underneath a turbulent current cunningly awaits the unwary traveler. Seasoned hunters and fishermen have long respected the unpredictable river while at the same time reaping the harvest of its waters.

The story goes that a group of white hunters was camped for the night on the shore of the river. The woodsmen had been on the trail for days and were camping their last night before heading back to their families with much-needed venison and bear meat, already dressed out. They were weary and trail-worn, but they still kept a constant alert for wildcats, which were known to drop from trees and tear their unsuspecting victims apart. Perhaps their greatest fear was of being attacked by a roaming band of Indians.

It was almost dark when the hunters began roasting fresh deer meat over their campfire. It was a cold, clear night, and when they had eaten their fill and settled down for some rest their conversation turned to the Phantom of the Forest.

One of the hunters told of actually having seen the Phantom. He believed the Phantom looked like an ordinary man—an ordinary man endowed with superhuman strength. Another hunter argued that he had seen the Phantom, and that the Phantom was seven feet tall with a black, bushy beard that reached to his waist and eyes that blazed as red as coals from a fire. The hunters argued back and forth about the appearancc of the Phantom, but they were uniformly grateful for him, for he had saved many settlers from the terrors of the Moratocs.

The hunters did not know it, but their own village, a scant few miles away, was being attacked by the Moratocs at the very moment they were idly speculating about the Phantom. Some of the settlers were killed and their homes and barns burned. Others were fortunate enough to escape into the woods or hide in cellars.

The particular band of Moratocs involved in the raid was notorious for taking captives to be used as slaves, which was a fate worse than being murdered outright. On this raid they chose several of the strongest and most able-bodied women for that purpose. They tied the women's hands behind them and forced them to march toward the Indian encampment, which was some distance away.

Their march took them directly toward the camp of the hunters. Daylight was barely beginning to filter through the dense canopy of trees when the Indians saw the faint reddish glow of a campfire. They hastily tied their captive white women to trees and left one young brave to guard them and keep them quiet. Then they stealthily advanced on the slumbering hunters.

The women later told what happened next. The forest was still and silent, broken only by the occasional hoot of an owl. They heard a slight rustle of leaves and felt a breeze stir up from nowhere. Suddenly their hands were untied, and their Moratoc guard slumped to the ground in death, his throat slit by an unseen hand. The women were stunned into silence by their ordeal of the previous night and by what they had just seen. As they huddled together the shape of a man appeared in the morning mist. He never allowed the women to fully see him, but he whispered for them to return as quickly as they could to their settlement.

The Phantom of the Forest then went quickly on the trail of the Moratocs. Just as the Indians were preparing to attack the unsuspecting hunters the Phantom leaped in front of them, eyes blazing, a knife in each hand and one between his teeth. The Indians fled into the woods screaming in terror, for they stood in total fear of the Phantom. The Phantom then disappeared as silently as he had arrived.

The hunters, roused by the noise of the fleeing Indians, quickly broke camp. They headed for the village, fearing the worst. Along the way they caught up with the women, who told them of the events of the preceding night. As they returned to their homes in the early light of morning they found a scene of pillage, death and destruction. But they knew how much worse it would have been if not for their protector, the Phantom.

During the following months the diligent settlers

worked together to rebuild their homes and barns and businesses. The story of the Phantom continued to spread up and down the Roanoke, until he became recognized as the best defense that the small communities had against the Indians.

It has been over a hundred years since anyone has reported sighting the Phantom of the Forest along the Roanoke River. The passage of time can diminish the power of a legend in the minds of some people, and there are those who will tell you that the Phantom is gone for good, or that he never existed at all. But there are others who insist that his presence in the forest is as strong as ever. Those people say that the Phantom is merely watching and waiting, and that when the time comes that someone in danger needs his help he will prove as potent an ally as he was in the days when the Indians feared his name.

6 | *Charlotte,*
Ghost of Somerset

f you follow U.S. 64 eastward toward Manteo and Nags Head you will pass through the small community of Creswell. The town's Main Street is situated well off the highway. It offers a few small stores and a soda shop, where visitors can quench their thirst. At the end of Main Street is a sign directing travelers to Pettigrew State Park, Lake Phelps and Somerset Place, which are located seven miles south of Creswell. Lake Phelps, the second largest freshwater lake in North Carolina, is well-known by fishermen throughout the state. Somerset Place, the antebellum home of the Collins family, is a state historic site furnished with nineteenth-century antiques. It is open for guided tours seven days a week. This story is focused around Somerset Place and its surrounding plantation.

In days gone by the part of Washington County where Somerset Place is located was known as the

Eastern Dismal, in reference to the Great Dismal Swamp along the North Carolina–Virginia border. The Eastern Dismal was an area shrouded in mystery. It was virtually unexplored by white men. Tales of gigantic beasts that roamed the dense virgin forests and snakes that slithered freely through the twisted undergrowth served to keep many would-be explorers away.

Although people lived in and around the Eastern Dismal they were content to leave its innermost secrets to the Indians and the wild animals. It was only by accident that the sixteen-thousand-acre Lake Phelps was discovered by a group of hunters.

The morning of August 23, 1775, was misty and hot. The group of hunters had been out for days, pushing deeper and deeper into the unexplored swampland. On that particular morning one of the group spotted a deer, and he and his mates gave pursuit. The big buck led them on a chase, and being clever in the ways of the swamps it soon disappeared from sight. The hunters tramped through the marsh trying to pick up the deer's trail, but without success.

They were about to give up and turn back, but one member of the group, a stalwart young man named Benjamin Tarkenton who hated to admit defeat, climbed a tree in a last effort to see the fleeing deer. What he saw was not a deer but a magnificent body of water that later proved to be eight miles wide. He promptly shouted back to his friends and told them of his find. Josiah Phelps, another member of the party, lost no time in rushing through the woods and falling to his knees in the shallow water, from which position he named the lake after himself. So it is that the massive body of water is called Lake Phelps to this day.

Some members of that adventuresome group succeeded in gaining title to portions of the land bordering the lake, but the tracts were virtually useless to them. The lake could only be reached by foot through dense woodland, and the cost of building a road to it was entirely unaffordable. The Eastern Dismal thus remained secluded and intact for a few more years.

All of that changed when the property came into the possession of a group from Edenton known as the Lake Company. It was in the late 1780s that the Lake Company had a canal dug between Lake Phelps and the Scuppernong River. The canal, six miles long and twenty feet wide, was dug entirely by slaves. The Six-Mile Canal, as it was called, permitted transportation into the Eastern Dismal for the first time. The slaves later excavated an intricate system of canals and ditches and built control gates that permitted the land to be alternately drained and flooded for the purpose of growing rice.

Josiah Collins of Edenton, one of the members of the Lake Company, became the sole owner of the property in 1816. He organized a plantation and named it Somerset in honor of Somersetshire, the county in England where he was born. When he died in 1819 the property was left to his son, Josiah Collins II, with the stipulation that it was subsequently to be divided into seven sections and distributed to the seven children of Josiah the son—the grandchildren of Josiah the father. Josiah Collins III, the eldest grandson, was to receive Somerset Plantation proper, while his brothers and sisters were to receive undeveloped lands.

It was for Josiah Collins III that the Greek Revival mansion called Somerset Place was built. Slave artisans constructed the house of hand-cut cypress and set it among stately oaks and cypresses. Somerset Place has since survived the Civil War, in addition to hurricanes and personal tragedies. Today, standing on a mere handful of the hundred thousand acres of the original plantation, it is a monument to the craftsmanship of a bygone era.

There are many legends and mysteries surrounding Somerset Place, but there are probably more stories about Charlotte Cabarrus than any other individual who has lived on the premises. Charlotte has been dead for over a century, yet her presence and influence are still keenly felt in the Collins mansion, where she lived for over half her life. There are people who say they have seen a mysterious light on the second floor late at night, a light that illuminates the shadow of a tall, thin woman wearing a bandanna and holding a wavering candle in her thin, bony hand. Others claim to have heard a baby crying, sometimes a muffled cry and other times a high-pitched scream like that of a newborn infant. A few declare that they have heard Charlotte's sobs echoing from her third-floor bedroom—deep, anguished cries of a soul racked with sorrow and misery.

It is a mystery why Charlotte's spirit remains so much a part of Somerset Place. No one has ever explained why she, a free black, was bound so firmly to Josiah Collins III and his wife, Mary, that she chose to stay with them in seclusion—raising their children and living her life through theirs—even though she could have chosen another kind of life.

The story of Charlotte Cabarrus began in Edenton in 1800, the year of her birth. Charlotte was born into slavery, the daughter of a black woman and a white man. When she was two years old her mother, Rose, gave birth to a son. It was said that brother and sister shared the same father. She may have been born a slave, but the light-skinned Charlotte was not destined for a life of slavery. In 1808, when she was eight and her brother was six, they were freed by their owner for unknown reasons.

Edenton in the early 1800s was a thriving port and the center of cultural and political activity in the area. Josiah Collins III was born the same year that Charlotte Cabarrus received her freedom. They grew up just a few blocks apart, as Josiah spent his childhood at the Homestead, the town house kept by the Collins family.

Josiah was eleven years old when his grandfather died. He was destined to bear the responsibilities that came with a sizable inheritance, so his education was given high priority. He attended Harvard before graduating from a law school in Connecticut.

The magical year in young Josiah's life came when he was twenty-one. Not only did he complete law school that year, but he also came into his inheritance and married his sweetheart, Mary Riggs of New Jersey. He and his bride moved directly to Somerset to await the completion of their mansion. It was after the birth of their first child when Josiah returned to Edenton and hired Charlotte Cabarrus to come and take care of the baby. Her salary was one hundred dollars per year.

Why did he not simply bring one of the family's slaves to the house to perform those duties? The answer involves both the laws concerning slaves and the lifestyle of the Collins family. There were Northern states that did not allow slave owners to cross their borders with slaves. Because Mary was a Northerner by birth the Collins family traveled north quite often. A sensible solution was to hire a free black who could travel with them and care for the children. Charlotte, known to Josiah from his days in Edenton, was the perfect answer to the problem.

It was sometime after 1830 when Charlotte came to Somerset Place. As she crossed the choppy waters of Albemarle Sound, disembarking at Mackeys Ferry for the long, bumpy ride to Lake Phelps, she could not have known that she would never call Edenton home again. She could not have known that she was destined to spend the rest of her life at Somerset Place in an existence where she was neither black nor white, neither slave nor her own master.

The third floor of Somerset Place was Charlotte's domain. Her bedroom for thirty years was a spartan cubicle tucked under the eaves at the head of the stairs. Just a few feet away was the large, airy, high-ceilinged room set aside for the children. It was an enchanting room, with plenty of space to romp and a window overlooking the lake.

Charlotte was always at the beck and call of the Collins children, for Josiah and Mary eventually had six sons. Charlotte was not just a nursemaid to the boys. She was also their friend. They loved and admired their mother, but it was to Charlotte that they went with their troubles and secrets and dreams. When they were sick it was Charlotte who sat with them until they were better, just as it was Charlotte who tucked them in at night and heard their prayers.

Her responsibilities went beyond caring for the Collins children. Charlotte dispensed quinine to sick slaves and made herself available for whatever tasks the lady of the house assigned. She was a paid worker, and Josiah Collins had a reputation for getting his money's worth from his employees.

Charlotte's new life at Somerset was a drastic change from what she had known in Edenton. She must have questioned her decision to leave the busy port town in favor of a place accessible only by poor roads and travel by boat. Edenton was home to a large population of free blacks, but Charlotte was the only free black at Somerset Place, a status that immediately set her apart.

The early years on the plantation were busy but peaceful. It was in February 1843 that tragedy first struck, snuffing out the lives of two of Charlotte's charges. Little Edward Collins was only eight years old and his brother Hugh ten that frigid day when their small boat overturned in the Six-Mile Canal.

Charlotte was busy tending to the current crib baby and was unaware of the tragedy happening to two of her beloved boys. It was sometime after four-thirty in the afternoon when Jim, a slave of the Collins family's nearest neighbors, the Pettigrews, spotted the capsized boat. He called for help and then ran to the bank of the canal, accompanied by Mr. Fitzgerald, the minister at Somerset Place. The water was frigid. Both slave and minister tried valiantly to rescue the boys, but it was to no avail.

The lifeless bodies of Edward and Hugh were

brought to the mansion and placed on separate beds. The fires in the house were built up to maximum intensity while the boys' bodies were rubbed in the vain hope of restoring life. When all hope was exhausted the corpses were removed and shrouded for burial. It is unknown whether Charlotte was called upon to perform that last earthly chore for the little boys she had lovingly raised.

The third floor of the house must have seemed terribly empty to Charlotte after the accident. Her days were busy enough tending to the remaining Collins children and the children who came with visiting relatives, but two of the voices that had been such a part of her life were now sorely missed. She would never again hear the footsteps of Edward and Hugh racing up the stairs or feel their arms around her neck when she tucked them in at night. She retired to her small room at the end of every day with a loneliness that could not be shared. She lay in her bed and grieved for her boys.

The years moved swiftly for Charlotte and the Collins family. Charlotte was not totally isolated at Somerset Place, for she accompanied the family to care for the children when they traveled during the summer months. Long Island and Saratoga Springs were among the places they visited, along with another family plantation, which was called Hurry Scurry. Somehow life seemed more tranquil when they were away from Somerset Place.

Somerset Place was destined to be the site of even more tragedy and unhappiness in the late 1850s, for another son of the Collins family was marked for an early death. This time the carriage drive was the scene of the accident. Once again death came in plain view of the house. William Kent Collins was riding his horse up the carriage drive at a full gallop when the horse stumbled and the young man was thrown against an elm tree. He died instantly. Josiah was so grieved over the death of a third son that he had a heavy chain fastened around the enormous old elm, which slowly cut into the tree and eventually strangled it to death. Charlotte felt as if she were being strangled, too. The new death was as painful to her as the loss of Edward and Hugh had been.

The Civil War brought the demise of two distinctly different ways of life that the South had known for many years. Slavery was ended, and the Southern aristocracy of wealthy planters saw its final days. Many formerly wealthy families were left with enormous debts. The Collins family was among them. Josiah died before the war ended, and Mary found herself in grave financial trouble. Her three remaining sons were unable to run the plantation profitably without slave labor. Mary eventually lost the Somerset property.

Throughout the war Charlotte remained with the Collins family, moving between Somerset Place and Hurry Scurry. When the children were grown she was given the position of housekeeper. Somerset Place had been her home for over half her life, and she chose to remain with the family whose heartbreak had been her own. She died at Somerset Place during the years following the war.

It was quite some time after the Civil War, when the house had been closed up and long-neglected, that the first of the stories of Charlotte's ghost surfaced. Some little boys who had been fishing at Lake Phelps overstayed their time and were caught by darkness. While taking a shortcut through the backyard of the Collins mansion they were surprised to see the faint glimmer of a light at one of the windows on the second floor. It disappeared as they watched, only to reappear in the window of Charlotte's third-floor bedroom. A shadowy figure moved back and forth in front of the tiny oblong window as the mesmerized children watched. After a few minutes the light was extinguished. The young fishermen had seen enough for one night and hurried home as though pursued by the devil himself.

Soon other residents began reporting mysterious lights at Somerset Place. Some witnesses saw the light of a single flickering candle that appeared to be held by someone who was pacing up and down the second-floor hallway. The light would come to a stop in front of one of the bedrooms. Then it would linger a few moments before continuing to the door of the next bedroom—back and forth, back and forth. Rumor had it that it was Charlotte traveling repeatedly between the two bedrooms where Hugh and Edward had been brought after their deaths.

In later years other reports told of not one candle, but three. The light in the middle, held higher than the others, was thought to belong to Charlotte, while those on either side were believed to be held by the ghosts of Hugh and Edward.

There are those who will tell you that they have heard sobbing and crying coming from a certain room on the third floor. It is in that room that the plaster will not stay on the chimney wall. The story goes that the plaster keeps falling because the body of Charlotte's baby is buried in the wall, though no one knows who fathered the child or when it was born or how it came to be laid to rest in a wall. Neither is it known for certain whether the cries are those of a mother or a newborn infant. Perhaps they are both.

Over the years there have been visitors to the now-restored mansion who have commented on feeling a distinct presence upon entering the third floor of Somerset Place. The aura is that of a deep, abiding sadness with no hostility or evil to it. Most people who have experienced it and who know the stories about the house are certain that it is the presence of Charlotte Cabarrus. Somerset Place was Charlotte's home for more than half her earthly life, and it seems that it is now her home for all eternity.

7 | *May She Rest in Peace*

Times were hard in rural North Carolina just after World War I. The Great War had thinned out the healthy crop of young men like a blight in a field of corn. Many of the country boys who set out confidently for the trenches never returned. Some who sidestepped death's talons left the fighting in faraway France with broken bodies or tortured minds.

In the early 1920s local farmers were struggling to make a living from the tired, overworked soil. Wives and children pinched pennies and did without all but the barest of necessities. Young people found their entertainment at church socials, corn shuckings, square dances and other such gatherings. For the most part children grew up and married within the community.

Occasionally a stranger would buy land and settle down in the northeastern portion of North Carolina. One such stranger was a handsome young bachelor from Raleigh. Speculation ran rampant for weeks as to why he had chosen such an out-of-the-way spot. More than one local resident believed that the stranger had been gassed in the war and had come to the country for his health. It was soon apparent that he was not destitute, and some of the more sinister-minded local citizens speculated that he had come by his wealth through shady dealings. But the stranger just went about his business of buying a farm and a team of horses, seeming not to notice that he was the star attraction wherever he went.

Mr. Johnny, as the stranger was called, soon began to receive his share of attention from the unmarried ladies. His pantry never lacked for cakes and pies and preserves. On Sundays he was never without invitations to dinner and supper. Mr. Johnny was considered quite a catch, and many a mother with unmarried daughters depleted her henhouse fixing his favorite meal, which was fried chicken. The young man's waistline must surely have expanded, for the story goes that he never turned down an invitation to a meal. Sometimes he had two dinners and two suppers in a day's time, all at different houses.

Time would prove that he was interested in more than just the food that those anxious mothers served. Mr. Johnny was nobody's fool, and he knew when he had played the field long enough and it was time to take a bride. He'd had his eye on two eligible maidens for quite a while. He would court Alice for a few days, and then Stella for a few days. Bitter feelings began to grow between the two girls, who had been the best of friends before Mr. Johnny arrived.

Alice had a sweetness and charm about her that Stella lacked. As Alice and Mr. Johnny saw more and more of each other people began to suspect that he had made his choice. Stella was heartsick, and in her despair she developed a mortal hatred for her old friend.

None of the local residents was what could be called wealthy, but it just so happened that Stella's father was more prosperous than most, as he owned the general store and a nice farm. He watched his only daughter grieve until she was thin and pale, and he just couldn't bear to see her so unhappy. So one night after he closed the general store he paid a call on Mr. Johnny. What took place between the two men that night was never publicly disclosed, but most people figured it out later. Suffice it to say that it was not the first time that money ever altered the course of true love.

The next afternoon Mr. Johnny paid a call on Stella. In a few days they were stepping out together, and sweet Alice was sad and teary-eyed. By the end of summer Mr. Johnny and Stella were married and Mr. Johnny was running his new father-in-law's general store. Tongues wagged and Alice cried, but Stella just smiled.

Stella had everything to make her happy, or so it seemed. Yet the truth was that she was purely miserable. Perhaps she had let her jealousy nag at her soul too long, but for whatever reason Stella's attitude toward Alice grew more bitter and vindictive every day. If she heard that Alice had been in the general store she would scream at Mr. Johnny when he came home at night and accuse him of still loving her rival. And on Sunday mornings when she encountered Alice at church she would stare relentlessly at her until the unfortunate Alice would leave the service.

Soon this violent hatred made Stella physically sick. Her father sent to the town of Rocky Mount for a well-known doctor. After the doctor examined Stella he diagnosed her illness as dropsy and told Mr. Johnny that she wouldn't live to see Christmas.

Stella knew she was dying. No amount of pleading could get her to eat, and her condition worsened by the day. Soon she was so weak that she could not get out of bed. Late one bleak November afternoon, as Mr. Johnny was sitting by her side, Stella asked him to promise her two things. The first was that he would bury her on the hill located in the middle of their peanut field and mark her grave with a tombstone of rose marble. The second request was the fruit of that evil seed called jealousy, for she made Mr. Johnny promise that he would never marry Alice. Deathbed requests are mighty hard to refuse, and Mr. Johnny hesitated only a moment before agreeing.

The doctor's prediction was right. Stella died just a few days before Christmas.

It was a gray December afternoon with sleet beginning to fall when she was laid to rest in the cold, red clay. Perhaps in his grief Mr. Johnny thought it would be fitting for Stella to be buried near the house. Some said he just didn't want to have to plow around a grave in the middle of his peanut field. The fact was that, for whatever reason, Stella was buried under the oak tree in the side yard, not in the field. Her grave was marked with a stone of rose marble, and the inscription read, "Rest in Peace, Faithful Wife."

Stella had made certain that several of her women friends knew about Mr. Johnny's promises, and when he broke the first one tongues began to wag. Everyone was guessing just how long it would be before he broke the second one.

After the burial Mr. Johnny locked up the house and went away for several weeks. Snow was on the ground when he came driving back down the road one January afternoon in a new black roadster. He didn't bother to go home first, but drove straight to Alice's house. It was after midnight when he unlocked his own front door.

Within a few days Mr. Johnny and sweet Alice were

being seen together. Gossip spread quickly, and it was rumored that a marriage would soon take place. The predictions proved correct, for on Easter Sunday they were married.

Mr. Johnny moved Alice into the same house where he and Stella had lived so briefly. He went back to farming and tending the general store, while she kept house. At first they were a happy couple, but then things began to go wrong. Alice would wake up in the middle of the night screaming that someone was trying to smother her or that she was being choked to death. Mr. Johnny would patiently light a lamp and sit beside her until she finally fell into a fretful sleep. Alice confided to her friends that she didn't feel safe in the house when Mr. Johnny was at work.

Some mysterious and unexplainable incidents began to take place. One morning when Alice was making up the bed she found a gold locket containing Stella's picture. When she confronted Mr. Johnny with it he was so upset he could hardly speak, for he was certain that the locket had been buried with Stella. Another day Alice came home from visiting a friend and found her china broken to bits on the dining-room floor.

Alice, who had always been a sweet and trusting girl, became withdrawn and nervous. She continued to be afraid to be alone in the house. Every day when Mr. Johnny went to work she left home and went to her mother's.

Mr. Johnny didn't let on to Alice just how worried he was about the whole situation. He finally decided that he and Alice should take a trip. He was hoping that a change of scenery would have a healing effect on their frayed nerves. Alice received his suggestion with more excitement and delight than she had shown since the first days of their marriage. She packed their trunks with the enthusiasm of a young girl, and her pale, drawn face began to regain some of its former rosy color. She was happier than she had been in a long time, and that just naturally made Mr. Johnny happy, too.

On the morning of their scheduled departure Mr. Johnny left early to go down to the general store to take care of some last-minute business. Alice decided that she would ride her little mare over to her mother's to say good-bye. It is uncertain exactly what happened, but just as Alice turned the corner in front of her mother's house she was thrown from her horse and her neck was broken.

There were whispers among the neighbors that Stella's ghost was responsible for Alice's untimely death. Some even claimed to have seen a woman in a white dress step out from behind a tree just before the accident occurred. They swore that the woman looked just like Stella.

Once again Mr. Johnny was a widower. He was inconsolable in his grief, for he had truly loved his Alice. His friends were so concerned that some of them stayed with him around the clock until the time of the funeral. Alice was laid to rest in a grave beside Stella's. The gleaming white marble of her tombstone glistened above the red clay of the freshly dug grave. Inscribed on the stone were the words "Beloved Wife."

A few days after the funeral Mr. Johnny went out to the graves to place fresh flowers on them. Everything was fine at Alice's grave, but he found a gaping hole at Stella's resting place. He was so horrified and frightened that he quickly filled the grave with fresh dirt and hurried back inside.

The following Sunday when Mr. Johnny visited the graves the gaping hole was back in Stella's grave, only it was much larger this time. The dirt that had come out of the hole was nowhere to be seen. Once again he filled the hole with a trembling hand and went home to spend a sleepless night in worry and dread.

The next morning he knew that he should go and check the graves, but all day he stayed away from the gruesome little cemetery, trying to put it out of his thoughts. On Tuesday morning curiosity overcame dread. Mr. Johnny went reluctantly to the site. As soon as he arrived his eyes grew wide with horror and a scream stuck in his throat, for he saw that Alice's stone had been broken in half and its inscription scratched completely out. This time all of the dirt had been thrown from Stella's grave and her tombstone was gone. Mr. Johnny wanted to believe it was the work of vandals, but in his heart he knew otherwise.

He made his way cautiously to the little hill in the middle of the peanut field, the hill where Stella had requested she be buried. There he found her tombstone sitting upright in exactly the spot where she had told him to lay her to rest. Early the next morning he had her coffin moved to the hill, and from that day on Stella rested in peace.

Mr. Johnny lived to be an old man. No one ever learned of his past before he came to northeastern North Carolina. He was considered quite a catch to the end of his days, but he never married again. At the time of his death he was buried beside sweet Alice—at his request.

8 | *The Mystery Lights of Tyrrell County*

ight is electromagnetic radiation, a source of illumination. The sun, an electric lamp, daybreak—all are explainable sources of light. But what about those means of light that cannot be explained, those lights that are apparently there but really aren't?

The story of the early efforts at colonizing what are now North Carolina and its neighboring states is an interesting one. A charter for land in America was granted to the Virginia Company in 1606. King James revoked it in 1624, perhaps because he was upset with the company's leaders for moving too slowly in their colonization project.

James did not live long enough to have the pleasure of granting the land to another group. His son was crowned King Charles. Charles promptly granted the

New World territory between latitudes 31 and 36 degrees North to his attorney general, Robert Heath. It was first called the Carolana Grant, though the spelling was later changed to Carolina.

The reign of King Charles was a stormy one that ended when the monarch was beheaded in 1649. The next eleven years were filled with fear and sacrifice among those who were supporters of the rightful heir, the son of King Charles. Finally, in 1660, King Charles II attained the throne and acknowledged a debt of gratitude to those who had supported him during his years of struggle.

Charles II was not stingy with his rewards. He was king, after all, and as such he held the wealth of England in his control. There were eight men who had been particularly supportive during the years of turmoil, and they were not bashful about the prize they hoped to win for their role in bringing the exiled king to power. That prize was the Carolina territory.

In 1663 King Charles II granted the territory to those eight noblemen, who became the Lords Proprietors of Carolina. One of them, Anthony Ashley Cooper, was later to become the earl of Shaftesbury. Edward Hyde was a lawyer and a member of Parliament who had been loyal to both Charles I and Charles II. William Craven and George Monck, the duke of Albemarle, had both served in the army. Sir William Berkley and Sir George Carteret had each given sanctuary to members of the royal family in exile. John Lord Berkley was a dedicated supporter of the Crown who was eventually forced to go into exile himself. And the last of the eight, Sir John Colleton, was a faithful British subject living in the West Indies.

The area now known as Tyrrell County was part of the grant given to Anthony Ashley Cooper. The area was recognized for its beauty and serenity as early as 1680, when Captain Thomas Miller and Colonel Joshua Tarkenton navigated the Scuppernong River. Those two explorers were so taken with the bounty of the land that they called the region Heart's Delight. By 1690 Englishmen were living on the shores of the river, and cotton and tobacco farms were being carved out of the wooded land. The vast area was also called South Shore at one time, since it was situated on the south side of Albemarle Sound.

It was in 1729 that the General Assembly of the province met in Edenton to fashion a county out of the wild and beautiful acreage, and Tyrrell Precinct was born. The piece of land in question was 150 miles long and 50 miles wide. So massive was this one county that some years later it was divided into four separate counties.

The community of Elizabeth Town—now Columbia—was established in 1793. It was declared the county seat of Tyrrell County a few years later, at which time a courthouse was built. Columbia is a "sleeping beauty" of a town even today. Turn-of-the-century homes flank tree-lined streets, and neighbors have time to visit and drink lemonade on screened-in porches. Down at the town dock sailboats bob lazily on the Scuppernong River, patiently awaiting their owners' return. The loveliness of the town extends out into the county, the peacefulness broken only by the drone of vehicles on U.S. 64.

Tyrrell County is crisscrossed by a wealth of secondary roads that lead the unsuspecting traveler to weather-beaten farmhouses and meandering streams crossed by wooden bridges. They also lead to cemeteries filled with the old dead and the newly deceased. In days gone by, long before perpetual-care cemeteries came into being, people buried their loved ones in community graveyards or in family cemeteries located in fields near their homes. Hundreds of those reminders of man's inescapable destiny are dotted across our rural landscape. It was at one such family cemetery that the Mystery Lights of Tyrrell County were sighted.

Shortly after supper one night a Tyrrell County farmer and his wife were sitting on the wide front porch of their two-story farmhouse with some of their neighbors. A slight breeze was stirring from the direction of a nearby creek, and that was the only thing that made the torrid summer night bearable. There wasn't much conversation, just the buzzing of the ever-present mosquitoes and the squeak of the rusty porch swing as it moved to and fro. Off to the south side of the house was the family graveyard, where the graves were kept safe from wandering cattle and hogs by a picket fence. Over the years a number of neighbors had been buried within the shelter of the frail, leaning fence, so that the graveyard had become more of a neighborhood resting place than one reserved for just a single family.

A child was the first to take notice of a light that appeared to hover over one of the graves. It was a shimmering ball of brilliant light about the size of a peck basket. Armed with nothing more than fortitude and curiosity the entire population of the porch advanced upon the graveyard. The light continued to flutter over that one particular grave until the inquisitive onlookers entered the gate, at which time it abruptly disappeared. A diligent search produced no evidence that anything out of the ordinary had taken place. The farmer and his wife and neighbors returned to their porch chairs without being able to offer an explanation of what they had seen.

Early the next morning a man in the neighborhood died. The group that congregated on the porch speculated on the events of the previous evening, and it was agreed by all that it was the tombstone of the deceased man's wife over which the mysterious light had shone. In due time the man was buried beside his mate.

Sometime later the strange light appeared again.

This time it shone so brightly that the names and dates on the tombstones could be read. Once again several curious observers advanced on the burial ground to try to discover the source of the light. As they entered the graveyard the light flickered and went out. Late the following afternoon a young woman who lived nearby was found dead.

People began to say that the light was an omen of death. The nights on the porch began to take on an atmosphere of dread. Some called it the Doom Light, while others spoke of it as the Death Light. Both names were spoken in hushed tones. The neighbors averted their eyes from the two fresh graves in the cemetery and tried to talk about the living rather than the dead.

When the light appeared a third time the people feared the worst. No one tried to discover its source this time, so the light remained visible until daylight. Before the night was out a child in the neighborhood who had been ill from typhoid fever finally died.

The neighbors mustered all their courage and began a nightly watch for the mysterious light, but their fears were for naught, as the light was never seen in the little family plot again.

In later years, when friends and neighbors gathered on that same porch to catch the elusive summer breeze and talk about the crops or the weather or grand-children, it was only natural that someone would bring up the time when he or she saw the Death Light. Children too young to remember the unexplainable deaths went from rowdiness to quiet submissiveness whenever the old folks began to tell the story.

When the Mystery Lights of Tyrrell County left for good the old burial plot held three new mounds of fresh dirt. It is not known to this date whether the local citizens were really given three warnings of approaching deaths, or whether the mysterious illumination meant something else altogether. Some said the lights were phosphorescence, while some said they were the product of marsh gas. Others called the whole episode just plain superstition. The only thing that can be said for certain is that the lights have never been explained, and probably never will be.

9 The Coach of Death

The area where Plymouth is located was settled by 1727, and a town was firmly established by 1790. The town grew rapidly in importance as a commercial center, thanks in part to its excellent location on the Roanoke River.

About three miles southeast of Plymouth is an area of rich farmland and cypress-filled bogs known as Garrett's Island. Garrett's Island is surrounded by swamps and intersected by meandering Conaby Creek, but it is not an island in the true sense of the word. There is a disconnected aura about the place, as if it is somehow different from the fields that join it to the remainder of Washington County. It is not surprising that Garrett's Island has been the site of eerie goings-on for many years.

King George II granted the tract that was to become Garrett's Island to John Corprew of Tyrrell County in 1746. The tract was first called Oval Island, then Bailies Island. It was later sold to Joseph Garrett, and it was at that time that it became known as Garrett's Island. At Joseph Garrett's death the property was passed to his son Alfred F. "Alf" Garrett and his daughter Harriet.

The Garretts constructed their family home on a hundred-acre farm. The Island Home, as they called it, is the oldest structure in Washington County. The gambrel-roofed house is two stories high, with a porch supported by hand-carved posts running across the front. The iron nails that still bind the structure together were made by a local blacksmith. The Island Home is a country house in every sense—it is stable, secure, serene and comfortable.

Alf Garrett was a familiar and well-respected figure on the dusty streets of Plymouth during the middle part of the nineteenth century. He kept a fine home within the town limits, where local political leaders often came to dine and to discuss the future of the thriving little river port. During the summer months he moved his family out to the Island Home, which provided a cool respite from the closeness and the steaming heat of Plymouth. The family could relax on the long front porch and just enjoy the quiet of the countryside.

Alf Garrett was a man of varied interests. In town he was a businessman, while in the country he was a gentleman farmer. For pleasure he indulged in a hobby he dearly loved—raising horses. Lake Phelps was a popular racing ground, while nearby Somerset Plantation had the finest race track in the eastern part of North Carolina. Garrett's horses raced at those two sites with the best the state had to offer.

Then came the Civil War. Alf Garrett and many other local residents joined the Confederate army. Garrett, nearly sixty years of age by then, was awarded the rank of major. He was fondly referred to as "Major Garrett" for the rest of his life.

Plymouth suffered greatly during the war. Few of the older houses in town were left standing. Major Garrett's home was among those burned. It was then that the family made the Island Home its permanent residence. They moved the possessions they had managed to save from the fire and for the next quarter of a century lived at Garrett's Island. The scant three miles between Plymouth and the island provided some measure of safety, though the family could still hear the sounds of fighting around the village.

During the war years Union soldiers roamed the countryside in search of food and clothing. Not all of the Union troops were unfamiliar faces, for some of the residents of Plymouth fought for the North. The town remained under the control of Federal forces until April 1864.

At the close of the war there were only eleven buildings left standing in Plymouth. The destruction of the main portion of the village meant that many who had previously earned a living in town had to turn to farming for their livelihood. So it was with the Garretts.

The peacefulness of the Garrett's Island countryside contrasted sharply with the blackened, burned-out corpse of the village, and the family was seldom without visitors. An invitation to a late-evening supper at the Island Home was a special delight. Such occasions were always well-attended. It was during one of them that the infamous Coach of Death made its first appearance.

The lengthy dirt road that led up to the Island Home was lined on both sides with cedars and crape myrtle. It was known as the Avenue of the Cedars. On the night in question a great many guests came to celebrate with the Garretts. They were greeted by candles sparkling in every window of the Island Home as their carriages rounded the bend in the Avenue of the Cedars. Music from a harpsichord floated on the cool night air as they alighted from their carriages and horses. The hospitable Major Garrett greeted his friends at the door and invited them inside to enjoy the warmth and hospitality of his gracious country home.

As the last guest entered and was being shown into the dining room Major Garrett turned to close the heavy wooden door behind him. He was surprised to hear the sound of horses approaching the house. The sound seemed distant, so he strained his eyes to look down the Avenue of the Cedars, wondering who it might be, for he knew that all of his invited guests were safely inside. The sound faded, and he could then neither see nor hear anything. He stepped out of the noisy house and onto the porch to listen intently, but he could hear nothing other than the sound of his deerhounds baying at the moon.

He was about to turn and go back into the house to join his guests when he heard the sound of carriage wheels and the pounding of horses' hooves in the avenue. Approaching the house at top speed was a coach of solid black, pulled by six jet-black horses. The coachman sat high in the driver's seat, and the reins that strained in his mighty hands shimmered like silver in the glow of the full moon. The air became noticeably cold and clammy as the coach drew up in front of the house.

Major Garrett was quite unnerved by the unearthly appearance of the coach. He took a step backwards and looked up to see if he could recognize the driver of the malevolent conveyance, but the driver's face was hidden in the shadow cast by his hooded cape. No sound came from the coachman or from whatever persons occupied the coach.

Someone called out to Major Garrett from inside the house, and he turned briefly to answer. The coach and horses had disappeared into the night by the time he turned back. He noticed that the air around the porch was no longer cold and clammy.

Major Garrett returned to the welcoming candle-light of his dining room. His guests had already gathered around the oval dining table, and as they saw the look of horror on his face the cacophony of chatter dwindled to total silence. Major Garrett feared that no one would believe him, so he hesitated before finally telling of the unearthly specter he had just witnessed. An air of uneasiness prevailed for the remainder of the evening, and the guests departed unusually early.

That night Major Garrett sought the solace of his bed, but he could not manage to find comfort in sleep. He had in his travels heard tales of a phantom coach that brought warnings of disaster and death. He could only hope that what he had witnessed was not the same.

Before the sun brightened the morning sky Major Garrett was roused from his bed by a thunderous knocking on the front door. He opened the door with more than a little trepidation, only to find a messenger bearing the sad news of a death in the family. It was then he was certain that the apparition of the night before had indeed been the Coach of Death.

In the ensuing years the Coach of Death came up the Avenue of the Cedars again and again. More than one family member beheld the ghastly apparition, and sadly enough it always foretold a death in the family.

The Island Home, like all old houses, has seen its share of births, deaths and war. The cedars and the crape myrtle are gone now, and the road no longer leads to the front door, but rather alongside the house. Across the road from the house is the graveyard of the Garrett family. The simple little cemetery is enclosed by a low brick wall and bordered by a sandy field. All is peaceful and serene now, just as it should be.

It has been nearly a century since a member of the Garrett family last witnessed the Coach of Death, but Garrett's Island has been the site of other unexplainable occurrences.

For many years hunters and residents of Garrett's Island told of seeing a white doe in the fields surrounding the Island Home. It was usually in the late afternoon, when the sun cast its last pinkish glow across the sky, that the doe could be spotted peacefully nibbling grass or peanuts at the edge of the fields. The deer was said to be pure white and quite small and delicate. Curious persons would sometimes try to draw close, but the deer would move toward the woods and seemingly fade away into the dense growth. It seems strange, but it is said that no one ever tried to shoot the white doe. Should anyone so much as attempt to kill the beautiful creature, the legend goes, a curse would be upon that person for the rest of his or her days.

The origin and meaning of the white doe are unknown, as is often the case with ghostly phenomena. The same can be said of one of the dearest but least-known ghostly manifestations witnessed at Garrett's Island, that of the Singing Children.

After the Civil War the Garretts cultivated their land with the help of tenant farmers, as did many other families with large landholdings. Sometimes the tenant farmers were paid a salary, but more often they farmed on shares. When the crops were sold and the bills were paid the tenant farmers received a certain percentage of the money that was left. Several small wood-frame houses of three or four rooms were erected on the Garretts' land. The houses were modest, but they were in many cases the first real homes the families had ever had, and they were glad to get them. Each tenant family had a garden and enough space to raise its own livestock, along with plenty of yard for their children to play in.

In the late 1940s a middle-aged bachelor and his spinster sister came to Garrett's Island as tenant farmers. They were given lodging in one of the frame houses. The house, unoccupied for some time, was a mess, and its yard was overgrown with weeds. But in a few weeks it seemed to be a different place, with the new tenants giving it lace curtains in the windows and a fresh coat of paint inside and out, along with a yard that was planted and raked to perfection. A vegetable garden was dug behind the house. All around the sturdy little home the sister planted dahlias and foxglove and gardenias and roses she had taken from her mother's home. The brother and sister thus made the arrangements that were designed to suit them for the remainder of their lives.

They had never been accustomed to much in the way of material goods, but they were gentle and wise. When they came to live at Garrett's Island it was with a sense of gratitude. Both brother and sister had a great respect for nature and its ways. They planted by the signs of the moon and doctored themselves and each other with healing herbs and potions. What they took from the land they gave back in double measure. They had a rapport with the little universe of Garrett's Island. Perhaps it is not surprising that they felt and heard things that more worldly people were never privileged to experience.

Both the Island Home and the cemetery of the Garrett family were within sight of the house shared by the brother and sister. After the last family of renters moved from the Island Home the sister would often walk down the dusty dirt road late in the afternoon to sweep the yard and water the ancient rose bushes and gardenias at the Garretts' old home. As often as not she'd pick a bouquet of flowers and arrange them in a jar of water before leaving them by one of the tombstones in the cemetery. Only when she was satisfied that all was well would she turn her gaze from the faded tombstones and return home.

It was late in the evening after one such excursion that the sister's attention was drawn to the old house, where she saw a light moving from window to window. The light, bluish orange in color, would disappear for a few moments and then reappear at the front windows. At times it flickered as though a breeze threatened to extinguish it, but then just as suddenly it would flare up again. Then the light disappeared altogether, and the Island Home was lost in the murky shadows of the giant trees. The sister watched for quite a while afterwards, straining her eyes in the darkness, but the light did not reappear.

The next morning brother and sister sat down to breakfast in a companionable silence, each pondering private thoughts, as was their custom. Afterwards the brother pushed his chair back from the table, removed his jacket and hat from their pegs by the door and said, "I'll be plowing in the cemetery field today, so don't look for me to come home till suppertime." With that remark he turned and was gone.

Energy was a commodity the spinster sister had in abundance. As she washed the breakfast dishes she planned her day's work. Her thoughts kept returning to the strange light she had seen the previous night. As the day wore on she worked in her garden and among her roses, but her mind often strayed to the flickering light. Late in the afternoon she fed her chickens and shut them up for the night, then walked back to the house to prepare the evening meal.

Supper was just being dished up when the bachelor brother came up the back porch steps. He stopped at the hand pump and scrubbed his face and hands and slicked down his hair before seating himself at the table.

Neither brother nor sister was given to flights of fancy. They were honest, hard-working people with their feet firmly planted in the dirt of Garrett's Island. But they had both lived long enough to accept the fact that there are happenings that no earthly being can explain.

For a few minutes they ate silently. Then quite suddenly the brother laid down his knife and fork and began to speak. "I've witnessed a mighty strange revelation this day, Sister," he said. He seemed hesitant at first, but then he continued. "I plowed all morning, and along about noontime I led the mule to the shade and gave him a bucket of water. That old mule had worked mighty hard. Since I was right there at the graveyard I decided I'd just sit down on the wall and open up my pail and eat a bite."

He hesitated again before saying carefully, "That's when I heard it the first time."

"Heard what, Brother?" his sister asked.

"Singing. I heard children singing. It was the sweet-est song I ever did hear. Sometimes it would fade away and they'd laugh and then they'd be up close enough for me to touch them, only I never could see them. It was the prettiest thing I ever heard, all soft and sad and sweet at the same time." As the brother talked his eyes had a faraway look about them.

His sister watched him thoughtfully for a time be-fore she asked, "What were the words they sang?"

"I don't know. It was just kind of nice and soothing. I tell you I couldn't see them, Sister, but I felt them all around me. It was a right comforting feeling, too."

So then she told him of the light in the windows of the Island Home. They talked about the phenomena they had witnessed, but they did not feel obliged to analyze the reasons for the flickering candle or the Singing Children, for they had seen signs and wonders before. It was time to go to bed when they finally rose from the table that evening.

The brother and sister witnessed other signs and omens during the years that followed, but never again did they see the light or hear the children. They never concerned themselves much with why they had been privileged to witness the occurrences, or with what-ever connection may have existed between the lights and the Singing Children. Neither did they concern themselves with what the Singing Children meant. They simply stored the beauty of the unexplained in their hearts, the benefit of that practice being that the mortal world held no terror for them.

Perhaps that is the best way to deal with ghostly visions and voices, for visions and voices, like the people who witness them, fade with the passing of time. The Avenue of the Cedars no longer resounds with the clip-clop of horses' hooves, and the dust from the old road has settled permanently under several inches of pavement. Tractors and trucks constitute the majority of traffic on the well-worn road today. The Island Home now stands empty, and the tenant house of the bachelor brother and his spinster sister is vacant, its windows covered by boards. No one around Garrett's Island has seen the Coach of Death or heard the Singing Children in many years.

10 | *The Rag Doll and the Knife*

hildhood is a precious and an all-too-short time. As children grow into adults they put the carefree and light-hearted days of their youth behind them, until childhood is just a memory. But not all the memories are pleasant ones. Some childhood memories might even be called haunting, for there are spirits so vile and evil that even innocent children are not safe from them. This is the story of one such example of evil.

Living in Beaufort County in the middle part of the 1950s was a girl named Caroline, as cute and friendly a six-year-old as there ever was. Caroline was an only child, so she was quite accustomed to inventing games and stories to entertain herself and her rag doll, Milly. Milly was Caroline's constant companion and the first "person" to be consulted about any new adventure. Caroline had found Milly in her Christmas stocking the year she was two years old. She had since received china dolls and dolls that walked and talked, but none was as dear to her as her old rag doll. Milly was now battle-scarred from constant love and attention.

Caroline's favorite among her many games was keeping house. Her grandpa had built her a tiny, one-room playhouse in the backyard, where she would entertain herself for hours on end. Her playhouse was her pride and joy. Whenever visitors came calling they first had to be shown the little house. Sometimes they were even offered a cup of pretend tea.

The playhouse offered many of the comforts of a real home. It had play versions of a sink and stove. Milly had a doll bed there, while Caroline had a white wicker rocking chair and a toy sewing machine. Occasionally Caroline's mother allowed her to borrow pots and pans and dishes from the kitchen. But there was one implement that Caroline was cautioned over and over never to use—the family's razor-sharp, long-handled butcher knife.

One summer afternoon Caroline, with Milly in tow, marched into her mother's kitchen for the purpose of borrowing the double boiler. She intended to make pretend fudge that afternoon, and the double boiler was an absolute necessity. There was no one in the kitchen to help her, so she pulled up a chair to reach the top of the pie safe, where her mother kept the pots. When she had the desired utensil in her arms she descended from the chair and gathered up Milly. Only when she was starting out the back door did she remember that she needed something with which to stir the fudge.

Caroline returned to the kitchen and opened the drawer where her mother kept the spoons and knives. Search as she might she could not find a big stirring spoon. But she did find the butcher knife. Caroline and Milly had a quick conference. They reasoned that if they intended the knife for stirring, rather than cutting, then it would be permissible to borrow it for a short time. A few minutes later they were in the playhouse stirring with the forbidden knife.

Caroline had every intention of returning the knife that afternoon, but good intentions have a way of going astray. She forgot all about the knife when her mother called her to supper. She finally remembered it while she and Milly were eating, but she knew that her mother would discover what she had done if she tried to go out after dark and bring the knife back. Caroline consoled herself with the promise that she would retrieve the knife in the morning and put it back where it belonged and never borrow it again.

The house where Caroline and her family lived had two stories. Caroline's bedroom was upstairs at the end of a long, dark hall. That night after supper she went up to her room. She always read Milly a bedtime story, so the two of them settled in side by side on their window seat with one of their favorite books.

Outside the sky got blacker and blacker, and a strong wind blew up. The curtains in Caroline's window were standing straight out by the time she finally decided to go to bed. Little girls and rag dolls rest well after a hard day's play, and the two friends were soon sleeping soundly, entirely unaware that evil was lurking nearby.

Caroline awoke with a start a little after midnight. The moon was shining through the window, so that grotesque shadows were performing eerie dances on the wall. She began to get frightened as she watched the strange forms twisting and writhing. She clutched Milly close and pulled the covers up around her head. Everything was quiet at first, but then she heard footsteps. From the direction of the stairs came a low, moaning voice that whispered, "I'm coming to get you, Caroline. I'm on the steps now." The steps squeaked under the weight of the intruder.

Caroline tried to scream, but no sound came out of her mouth. She was shaking all over. She rolled off her bed just as she heard the scratchy whisper say, "I'm coming closer, Caroline. I'm almost to your door now."

As Caroline crawled under the bed she heard the rattling of her doorknob, followed by the creaking of the old, stiff hinges as the door was slowly opened. While she lay on the cold floor a horrible thought came to her. In her haste to hide she had dropped her rag doll. Milly was still on the bed. Caroline thought briefly of scrambling out from under the bed long enough to rescue her companion, but there was no chance of that now, for she heard the sound of shuffling feet moving across her bedroom. She lay frozen in terror in the darkness, hardly daring to breathe while she strained her ears listening to the intruder's raspy breathing.

For a few seconds everything was unnaturally still. Then Caroline heard something hit the bed above her with a soft thud. It was only a few seconds after that when she heard her door being closed again, so softly that the old hinges didn't even creak. Then came the squeaking of the stairs as someone descended slowly and cautiously. So quiet was the house that Caroline could hear the latch on the front door as it opened and closed. But even then she was too mortally frightened to scream, or to rescue Milly and take comfort in holding her tight. All was still for the rest of the night, while Caroline lay huddled under the bed.

When the first murky light of morning finally dawned Caroline crept hesitantly from her hiding place. For a few seconds she remained flat on her stomach, ready to roll back under the bed if she heard any strange noises. Then she gathered all her courage and peeked over the edge of the bed.

Her reaction was one of horror. She started screaming, for there lay Milly—her rag doll and best friend— with the butcher knife deeply embedded in her chest.

Caroline's late-night visitor has never been identified. Neither is it known why the intruder chose such a horrible way to return the knife Caroline had left in her backyard playhouse. At first the story sounds like little more than the troubled dream of a girl who felt guilty about doing something contrary to a parent's wishes. But that hardly accounts for the specter of a rag doll with a knife stuck in its chest, for that part of the story was as real and unsettling as a little girl's screams.

11 | *Blood on the Floor*

he firing on Fort Sumter on April 12, 1861, began a terrible war that left a good deal of bitterness and mistrust in its wake.

A crucial day in North Carolina's history came on May 20, 1861, a little more than a month after the opening shots of the Civil War. That was the day the Old North State seceded from the Union. North Carolina went on to supply over one-sixth of the soldiers who served for the eleven-state Confederacy. By the time the war ended the Old North State had lost more men than any other Southern state. Even the most remote communities in the state were affected. North Carolina was changed forever.

The North's campaign was designed to capture Richmond, the capital of the Confederacy, then blockade the ports of North and South Carolina before finally dividing the South by taking control of the Mississippi.

The coast of North Carolina proved exceedingly difficult to defend. Even though several forts were established along the coast they proved unable to hold off the Northern onslaught. Thus it was that the Union army began to move inland to occupy the small coastal towns and villages.

Some coastal residents moved westward to Chapel Hill, Raleigh, Hillsborough and Pittsboro—places that were considered relatively safe. The majority of the people had no choice but to remain in their homes and defend themselves as best they could. There were also a few wealthy landowners who fled the coastal region, leaving their plantations in the care of relatives and slaves and returning only to conduct seasonal business. This story shows one sad result of the tensions between the occupying army and local residents.

It was a bitterly cold Saturday morning. The wind was blowing a mixture of ice and snow across Lake Phelps, whose waves were lapping against the brick foundation of Somerset Place, the beautiful home of the Collins family. Coming up the carriage drive were three Yankee soldiers—a captain, a lieutenant and a private. They leaned forward on their mounts, capes wrapped around their bodies in an effort to ward off the savage gale that was hitting them full force. They reined in on the north side of the house, away from the fierce winds tearing across the lake, in order to give the horses some protection from the winter storm.

The Union army was camped only a few miles away from Somerset Place. Soldiers were often seen on or around the plantation. The Collins family had been away during the previous summer, and the soldiers had received a warm welcome at the big house. But since the family's return in the early fall the hospitality—if it could be called that—had been formal and cool.

The captain and the lieutenant were intent on the business at hand, which involved Josiah Collins III, the owner of Somerset Place. It was never easy to deal with Collins, for he was a bitter enemy of the Union whose own sons were fighting for the Confederate cause. But since their encampment was located on the Collins property the Union officers had found it necessary to conduct a certain amount of business with the family. Neither the officers nor Collins relished the visits.

The young Union private also had business to attend to, but it was business of a different sort. His interest was the young Collins relative who had been living at Somerset Place since early summer.

How well he remembered their first meeting. His regiment had run short of supplies for both men and horses, and the captain had marched them toward Somerset Place, figuring it was the likeliest location in the region to have adequate supplies on hand. The enormous plantation was well-known for its wealth and abundance. It was also rumored that Josiah Collins III had gone to Hillsborough, making it more likely that his slaves would be willing to help the Union soldiers.

It just so happened that the private and two of his mates were wounded in a skirmish the day before they reached Somerset Place. At first the private thought his wound was minor, as the bullet had passed right through his leg. But the wound quickly grew infected, and he went out of his head with fever. That was when he first saw the girl. The captain had sent to Somerset Place for medicine for his wounded men. The girl and a Negro woman came with a basket of powders and quinine and clean bandages. The girl dressed his wound and sat by him for three days until the fever broke.

When he could finally sit up she fed him the first food he had eaten in days—some buttered toast and weak tea. He was in such poor condition that he could not talk, but when the girl gently held his hand he knew she was expressing more in that gesture than words could convey. He slept peacefully that night. The girl had returned to the house by the time he awoke.

For the next several days the private had looked forward to her return, and when she did not come back he very cautiously inquired about her from the slaves who came daily to the camp. Sensing a romance in the making they told him that the girl was a poor relation of the Collins family who had been sent to Somerset Place because she had nowhere else to go. It seemed that the girl had quickly become a favorite with the slaves and the house servants, as she was kind and good to everyone. The Yankee soldier's heart was touched by both her plight and her kindness to him. With the slaves as willing couriers he was able to exchange a few letters with her before the Union forces broke camp and moved on.

It was when the regiment returned a few months later that their love affair had begun in earnest. They knew that they were treading on forbidden ground, but they were very much in love, and rules and conventions had little meaning for them. With the help of others they began to meet secretly, exchanging letters when they couldn't see each other.

Even now, as he stood facing the icicle-laden formal garden of Somerset Place, the private could feel her eyes upon him. He knew without looking up that she was standing at her bedroom window watching him.

The captain and the lieutenant dismounted and strode toward the front porch, heads bent and shoulders hunched to ward off the wind and snow. Only then did the private lift his eyes to the upstairs window for a furtive glance at his lover. His breath caught in his throat, for it was not the girl who stood watching him, but an older woman who stared at him with unmasked hostility. The woman never took her eyes from his face as she slowly drew the heavy velvet curtains shut. It seemed as if she wished to memorize every feature about him.

A few minutes passed, during which the private shifted from one foot to the other in a vain effort to keep warm. Then he heard a tapping sound. At first he couldn't identify the source of the noise, but he soon realized that it was coming from somewhere above him. Looking up toward the very top of the house, sleet hitting him in the face, he could just make out a figure standing at the tiny half-window on the third floor. He knew it was his lover even though the distance was too great for him to see clearly. Suddenly a thought more chilling than the wind itself shot through his mind. He understood that the Collins family had discovered their secret, and that the girl had been exiled to a third-floor prison to keep her from loving an enemy soldier.

The private was unusually quiet when he got back to camp, for he was deeply affected by the sadness he had sensed about the girl at the window. His fellow soldiers teased him, saying he was a lovesick puppy who had fallen for a Southern belle. That night as he sat huddled by the campfire he experienced a strange feeling that he would never see his lover again.

The next few days passed slowly. It was the middle of the following week when the private received the bitter news.

He had been correct in supposing that the young girl was a prisoner on the third floor. The Collins family intended to keep her there until she came to her senses and gave up her Yankee lover. One of the servants brought her food at mealtimes, and that was the only contact she was allowed.

On the fifth day of the girl's confinement, as on the previous days, the servant climbed the steep stairs to the third floor, balancing a tray of food in one hand and fresh towels and linens in the other. But when she reached the top stair she immediately started screaming, for a puddle of blood was forming under the crack of the bedroom door, and a thin red stream was creeping across the floorboards.

The girl who was loved for her gentleness had died a violent death by her own hand. She was found face down in a pool of blood. Her wrists were cut to the bone, and her lovely face bore witness to the agony of pain and death. She was buried the next day in an unmarked grave, a mound of rich plantation soil the only sign that a body lay in the cold, hard earth. The Collins family ceased to mention her. It was almost as if she had never existed for them.

The Union private grieved alone for his lover. His comrades, feeling remorseful for having badgered him about the girl, tried to give him comfort. But nothing eased the pain in his heart, and night after night he could be seen sitting by the grave. A few weeks after the girl's death the regiment was moved to a Union encampment near Plymouth. The young private never returned to Somerset Place and its bittersweet memories.

When spring finally came that year the little grave no longer looked so naked. Grass had begun to grow over it, and a few wildflowers bloomed in the place where a headstone should have been. No one from the family ever visited, but occasionally a bunch of flowers was left by one of the slaves. It wasn't long before the incident was nearly forgotten.

The bedroom on the third floor went unused until fall, when some visitors were scheduled to come to Somerset Place. It was a rainy afternoon in early October when one of the servants ascended the stairs to clean the rooms on the third floor and get them ready for company. After a few moments screams began echoing through the mansion. Another worker rushed up the stairs to find the first servant terrified and incoherent. On the floor of the room where the suicide had taken place, in the exact place where the girl's body had been found, was a huge puddle of blood.

Once they regained their composure the two servants armed themselves with water and stiff brushes and started scrubbing the floor. In a short while the floorboards were entirely clean. But the blood seemed to have a mind of its own. It had to be scrubbed up time and time again over the next several months, as it always reappeared whenever there was a rainy day.

Eventually the servants refused to go into "the dead woman's room," as they called it. They got so tired of trying to cope with the recurring problem that they closed the room and locked it tight.

The Civil War was coming to an end, and the former slaves were leaving the plantation for new lives of freedom. There was hardly enough help to keep Somerset Place operating, and the third floor received very little use. The young girl's bedroom remained locked and unoccupied for many years.

Between 1872 and the late 1930s the Collins property changed hands a number of times. The house was lived in by a succession of tenants, and it was decided at some point that the third floor would once again be put to use. The key to the girl's bedroom was found, and the door was opened. There was a bloodstain on the floor.

The state of North Carolina acquired the property in 1939 and made it a state historic site thirty years later. Somerset Place was restored and furnished with antiques from the 1800s, including a few pieces that originally belonged to the Collins family.

Somerset Place continues to be a popular stop among history buffs and visitors to the area even today. Those who choose to take the house tour can go up to the third floor and check for bloodstains themselves. The floors and the rest of the home were thoroughly cleaned during the renovation, and they are cleaned periodically to this day, but it is doubtful whether even modern restoration and housekeeping methods can erase the legacy of the desperate young woman who took her life so many years ago.

| *The Spirit of*
Sweeten Water
Creek

he Martin County community of Griffin's Township is as lovely a place as you could ever hope to see. Gracious country homes with manicured yards sit serenely among hundreds of acres of farmland and majestic pine trees. The residents are warm and friendly. Many of them can trace their roots back two hundred years to the people who settled the area. Old-fashioned hospitality is extended to friend and stranger alike with a sincerity that makes visitors want to settle in and call the place home. There is an aura of peacefulness and safety that enfolds the little community.

But every so often that aura is broken, and the peaceful atmosphere is pierced by the screams of a young woman who died over a century ago. On cold, black, moonless nights a thick fog rises from the swamps to hang like a shroud over the murky waters of

Sweeten Water Creek. Traversing the creek near Griffin's Township and the community of Farm Life is a bridge that is haunted by the ghost of a beautiful young girl who died there under mysterious circumstances.

Water transportation was of the utmost commercial importance to the small communities along the Roanoke River during the eighteenth and nineteenth centuries. It was during that period that agricultural production in Martin County began to thrive. Tobacco, cotton, corn and livestock were carried down the creeks to the larger ports on the river. From there they were loaded onto large ships and transported to markets in the Northeast. Tar and shingles were among the other products shipped along the waterways. The numerous creeks that fed into the Roanoke were widely used for transportation and commerce.

One of the creeks so important to the livelihood of Martin County residents was Sweeten Water Creek. Stories abound as to the origin of the creek's name. One tale tells of a traveler who stopped to refresh himself and his horse at the creek. Upon taking a cold, delicious drink he declared it "sweetened water."

Another story concerns a farmer who went to Williamston to stock up on his monthly supplies. The farmer loaded his purchases in the back of his mule-drawn cart and headed back out toward his farm in the county. When he came to cross the creek one of the wheels fell off his cart, which caused its entire contents to spill into the creek. A large barrel of molasses broke open and trickled into the water. Legend has it that the farmer remarked, "Well, old mule, I reckon we've sweetened the water in this creek." From that day onward the creek has been called Sweeten Water Creek.

An old wooden bridge over Sweeten Water Creek at Griffin's Township provided the means for wagons, horses and foot traffic to cross the water. Near the bridge was the home of the Yarrell family, built by Matthew Yarrell in the eighteenth century. His descendants still occupied the home at the time of the Civil War, when the events of this story took place.

During the war years one member of the family was a young, beautiful girl who was by all accounts a bright spot in the life of the community. One of her greatest pleasures was to meander down to Sweeten Water Creek in the late afternoons and sit on an old cypress stump and watch the sun cast its last light of the day. She would dream her young girl's dreams about the boy she was engaged to and their plans for when he returned from the war. Neighbors crossing the bridge over the creek often saw her working on a quilt or crocheting a doily for her hope chest. But the girl's innocent dreams must have been touched with a measure of doubt, for she knew that many young men came home from the Civil War crippled in mind or body, and that some never came home at all.

One damp, cool evening the girl did not return home at the usual time. By dark her family was worried. They lit lanterns and went out to look for her, calling and searching. The moonless night, without even a lone star to use as a guide, greatly hindered their search. They returned home cold and exhausted, without so much as a trace of the missing girl.

There was very little sleep for anyone in the old Yarrell place that night. Coffee brewed on the iron cookstove all evening while the family gathered around the kitchen table, too sick at heart to sleep. Every so often one of them would light a lantern and walk down to Sweeten Water Creek and call out for the girl, hoping in vain for the answering voice that never came.

Late in the afternoon of the following day the girl's bruised and battered body was found entangled in a clump of cypress knees beneath the old wooden bridge. There was no clue as to how she had met her death. Some of her friends believed she had drowned herself, but there were others who suggested she had been murdered by a rejected lover.

It was a year to the day later, on a night as dark as a tomb, when a man crossing the bridge heard screams coming from somewhere underneath. The screams reached an ear-splitting pitch as he scrambled down the slippery embankment. Then they ended as abruptly as they had begun. The man called out, but the only reply was his echo reverberating among the pilings.

As he clambered back up the slope a movement at

the edge of the swamp caught his eye. In that one fleeting moment he beheld an apparition in white. He was terrified, but only for an instant, as the vision melted quickly into the shadows of the night. He was certain he had seen the ghost of the Yarrell girl.

As the years passed local residents continued to hear moans and screams coming from the bridge. Some described seeing a girl in white sitting on a cypress stump at the edge of the swamp. There were those in the community who grew unwilling to cross the bridge at night, especially if there was no moon.

The reports of strange sounds coming from the bridge over Sweeten Water Creek continue even today, and the ghost is still sighted in her customary place. Those who are brave enough, or foolhardy enough, to want to view the site can find the old bridge on State Road 1528 near the community of Farm Life.

There are two schools of thought as to why the young girl continues to haunt the bridge. Some local residents believe she is merely musing over her Civil War lover, as she liked to do in days gone by. That is the tame version. Others say there is darkness in her heart. They say she is biding her time, watching and waiting with evil intent should her murderer ever return.

13 | *White Feather*

e sat at her kitchen table as the rays of the late-afternoon sun filtered through the limbs of the giant pine trees. It was a typical midsummer day—hot, hazy and humid—but the air inside the house was cool and still. The only sounds that penetrated the soothing atmosphere were the clinking of the ice in our lemonade and the comforting hum of the air conditioner.

She had a story to tell, a story of a time when she, a modern-day woman, encountered a ghost from generations past. She spoke without hesitation of the bond she had discovered between herself and a long-dead Indian, a bond based upon the tragedy of lost love. Her story transported us to times past, to the days when White Feather roamed the banks of the Roanoke River.

The Tuscarora Indians were a powerful, fierce, proud tribe. They once lived and hunted and fished on the Bertie County side of the Roanoke in an area now known as Indian Woods, a forty-thousand-acre tract awarded to the tribe in 1717. King Tom Blunt, the chief of the Tuscaroras, had cooperated with Colonel Thomas Pollock in helping bring the Indian wars against white settlers to a close. The Indian Woods tract was the tribe's reward.

It was in that paradise of river and virgin forest, filled with fish and wild game, that a young Indian called White Feather grew to manhood. From the days of his childhood he hunted and fished and swam the Roanoke, roaming every inch of the Tuscarora lands. He knew the signs of the forest, the calls of the wild birds and the secrets of the animals.

White Feather had a manly beauty that was unmatched by any of the other braves. He was taller than his fellow Indians, and his arms and chest rippled with the sinewy muscles of a true athlete. His straight black hair hung to his shoulders, while around his forehead was a beaded band with a single long, white feather in it.

The Indian maidens were enchanted by the handsome brave. More than one of them secretly hoped that she might be chosen as his mate. The truth was that White Feather had already made his choice, but that no one in the tribe knew of it, for he kept his own counsel. There was a certain girl, the youngest daughter of the chief, who was more beautiful than anyone White Feather had ever beheld. She swam the river as gracefully as a deer and walked through the forest so softly that only the creatures to which she spoke knew of her presence. She had not only an outer beauty befitting a princess, but also a remarkable inner beauty. She was kind and gentle to both people and animals. Throughout the village she was respected as much for her healing powers as for her great beauty. It was said among the tribe that the chief's youngest daughter could heal wounds with her touch alone.

White Feather went to the chief when the young maiden was in her sixteenth year. He asked for permission to marry her. The chief was an astute man who was not altogether surprised at the request, but neither was he entirely pleased. He had already, in secret, promised his cherished child to another brave, and as the head of the tribe he could not go back on his word. The chief did not offer White Feather an answer, but told him he would give the request his careful consideration. White Feather was told to return in three days.

When the appointed time came the young brave received neither an answer nor a promise from the older man, but rather a challenge. He was told to accompany three other young Indians on a hunting expedition to distant parts. Upon his return he would be given an answer to his request. White Feather supposed that the mission was designed to test his manhood, so he departed with a light heart, confident that he could overcome any challenge and thus win his bride. Little did he know what was in the old chief's mind.

It was a month before the weary hunters returned, bringing with them many valuable animal furs. They entered the village to the sound of merriment. They soon came to understand that a marriage ceremony was taking place. White Feather was horrified to see that his young princess was the bride and that the chief was giving her to another brave.

He turned and walked away from the wedding, heading slowly and resolutely along the path to the river. Everything he had been dreaming of for years had just been wiped out in a few moments' time. His heart was loyal to only one girl, and spending a lifetime without her was unthinkable.

The path ended at a high bluff over the river. When White Feather's bare feet touched the crumbling red clay of the embankment he paused for just a second, then leaped into the rapidly running Roanoke with all the power in his young body. He fought every instinct to swim, allowing his body to sink under the foaming waters again and again, until he was no longer in control. Days later his broken and bruised remains were found many miles downstream, caught by a log near the shore. The white feather in the beaded band around his head was still whipping valiantly in the early-morning breeze.

It was not long after that when the Indians began to

tell of seeing the spirit of White Feather. He was usually witnessed in the late afternoon walking along the river. Then he would disappear as suddenly as he had come. White Feather never spoke, but those who encountered him always said that there was an air of great sadness about him.

The Tuscarora Indians eventually left Bertie County and relocated to New York State, where many of their kinsmen had set up homes years before. In 1831 seven Tuscarora chiefs met in Niagara County, New York, to sell all their rights to lands in Bertie County to the state of North Carolina.

Once in a while the story of White Feather would be told by someone from the Indian Woods section. On rare occasions it was reported that the young brave had been seen walking along the banks of the Roanoke, his feather blowing in the breeze. But as the years rolled by the stories grew less and less common and the memories of White Feather grew more and more faint, until he was all but forgotten.

Then came a day in the late 1960s, a time so far removed from White Feather's that there would seem to be no basis for a common ground spanning the years. But some things, like the tragedy of a broken heart, exist outside the boundaries of time. Sometimes a compassionate spirit from another age can make its presence felt if the summons is strong enough, particularly if someone is suffering the pain of lost love and is in need of comfort. On that twentieth-century day, when the United States was at war with a small Asian country thousands of miles away, the summons indeed proved strong.

There was a young woman who had lived on a farm in Indian Woods all of her life. She had grown up the only girl in a family of boys, and she could swim and hunt and fish and work on automobiles, but she was feminine, too. The girl had a strong Indian heritage. She loved the land and the animals and the seasons, and she knew every inch of woods and riverbank near her family's farm. In fact she was very much like the young Indian girl White Feather had loved so dearly so many years ago.

From childhood onward the girl had always sought refuge in the woods by the river in times when she needed consolation. So it was only natural that on the darkest day of her young life she should seek solace by the river's edge. She cried uncontrollably, for she had just learned that her lover would never return from the war taking place halfway around the world.

Time had lost its meaning for her, so she was unaware how long she had been at her private sanctuary when she suddenly felt that she was no longer alone. At first she thought that one of her brothers had come to aggravate her, or just to check and see if she was all right. But the silence continued, and she soon gave up that thought. She sat perfectly still for several moments, until she finally saw who it was who had come to her in her time of need. Standing tall and straight, with his feather blowing in the gentle afternoon breeze as he looked directly into her eyes, was the young Indian called White Feather.

It could have been moments or it could have been hours that they looked at each other like that. It was a time that could not be measured by the clocks of men. Finally White Feather raised his hand slightly and disappeared into the woods.

A sense of peace like none she had ever known before filled the young woman. The encounter had been fleeting, and not a single word had been spoken, but it was as if the Indian had given her the will to accept what had happened and the inspiration to go on with her life. There existed between White Feather and her a bond that could not be severed.

That heartbroken girl, a woman now, has never encountered White Feather again in all the intervening years. But she has not forgotten him.

14 | *The Little Red Man*

ome houses get a reputation for being haunted because folks claim to have seen lights or heard strange sounds emanating from within them. Other houses come complete with resident ghosts that some people can see and others cannot. But it is unique that a house should come equipped with a Little Red Man—not a friendly dwarf, but a vile and sinister creature who will stop at nothing to get his way. This is the story of such a house and its evil occupant.

About halfway between Jamesville and Williamston, the county seat of Martin County, lies an area known as "the Islands." Portions of the area's land are low-lying and crisscrossed by swamps, while other portions are high, well-drained, rich farmland.

The swamps are home to majestic old cypress trees. The ancestors of those same trees were the mainstay of the local economy in the period following the Civil

War. In those days cypress shingles were considered the finest and most durable roofing for houses. Almost every family in the Islands had at least one member who was employed in the shingle industry.

Back in the old days much of the land was owned by a single family, but tract by tract it slipped away from them. The high land was excellent for growing just about any crop from corn to soybeans. In the late nineteenth century tobacco was introduced in Martin County, and it, too, thrived on the rich soil of the Islands. Tobacco was a crop strictly for people who didn't mind hard work. Farmers loved to tell people that "the golden leaf" was their "January-to-December" crop, meaning that there was always work to be done. But there was also money to be made, and tobacco land in the Islands became more and more desirable for those who didn't mind the intensive labor.

The same soil that nurtured the golden leaf was ideally suited for a tastier crop—watermelon. There was one old resident of the Islands who was famous for his gigantic watermelons, which were bigger and sweeter than any others grown in the vicinity. When his crop was ripe the old man would load them on his mule-drawn wagon and head down the road singing, "Watermelon, watermelon, ripe to the rind. One for a nickel, two for a dime." Women and children would stand alongside the road waiting to choose the pick of the crop.

Since their region was so remote, with parts of it accessible only by boat, the Islanders were a law unto themselves. Just about everybody was kin to everybody else, so disagreements sometimes became especially heated. Old-timers still tell about fights and shootings and family feuds. It was a rare occasion when an officer of the law intervened. One way or another the Islanders managed to settle matters among themselves. They birthed their own, raised their own and buried their own.

Many local families were large. It was not unusual for more than one family to live under the same roof—parents, children, grandparents, nieces and nephews. Much of the land immediately around the houses was used for gardens, which the women and children were expected to plant and weed and hoe. The chicken yards provided both eggs and meat for the table. Fried chicken was a Sunday staple, and the henhouse was considered almost as important as the house where the family dwelt. It was a self-sufficient time, but that was not entirely by choice. For some there had never been another way, while for others it was simply a matter of necessity.

Then came a period so black that it touched the entire nation—every state, county and rural crossroads. That period was the Great Depression. Martin County fared no better than other rural areas in North Carolina. People who had lived moderately well became paupers because of the failure of the banks. Those who were already poor became destitute.

Country people came to one another's aid, even when they were down and out themselves. If they had something to share most of them did so. The general feeling was that no one knew when they would have to ask for help themselves. People were therefore willing to share food, clothes, fuel and housing whenever they were able.

It was a cold winter day during the Depression when a man named Dan and his wife and two children came knocking at the door of some relatives who lived in the Islands. The relatives' house was filled with children's voices and the sound of pots and pans being used in the kitchen, so it was not until the dog began barking that the door was finally opened.

The four people on the doorstep were in dire straits. Dan and his wife, Lizzie, were ill-clad for the frigid weather. Neither of them wore a coat, but only thin sweaters that did nothing to keep away the biting chill of the wind. Their two little children were wrapped in threadbare blankets. The four of them had traveled all day, hitching rides along the road with anyone kind enough to stop. They had walked between rides. The family owned an old rattletrap of a car, but with barely enough money for food there was nothing available for gasoline.

Dan had gone from job to job for months, taking

whatever employment he could get. Working hard for ten to twelve hours a day had earned him only enough to pay the rent on a miserable room and give his family the crudest kind of existence. Finally the last of the jobs had run out. They had no rainy-day savings to tide them over, for every day had been a rainy day for far too long. Only then did Dan put his pride in his pocket and go calling on his kinfolk down in the Islands. He knew that his aunt and uncle had little more than he did, but that they would not think of turning his family away whatever their circumstances.

Dan and his wife and children were welcomed into the living room and encouraged to thaw out by the fire. Dan talked to his uncle while the women dished up some hot food in the kitchen. Dan's thin face was creased with worry lines as he told his uncle about the hardships he and his family had endured. He was a proud man, and it did not come easily to ask for help, even from a relative.

The uncle reached over and patted Dan's hand. "Son, don't ever be too proud to ask your family for help," he said. "Times are hard all around. We ain't got much, but we've got enough so none of us'll starve. If you and Lizzie don't mind living in the old tenant house down the road you're welcome to it."

Dan felt his face flush a bright red, for gratitude was something that embarrassed him. He was unaccustomed to asking for help, but thanking someone for it came harder yet. "Me and Lizzie'd be proud to live in that old house where you and my daddy were born," he finally said. "And we'll take good care of it and pay you some rent just as soon as I get work."

"Son, I ain't too worried about the rent," his uncle said. "I used to rent that old place out, but in the last few years I've had no luck with renters. Folks'll come by and ask to rent it. Then I take them down there and show them around, and they seem right pleased. But first thing I know they up and move out and there it sets, empty again. I always did hate to see houses that are empty. They look kind of lonesome and forlorn to me. I'll be right glad for you to be down there. It'll be good for the old place." And with that the uncle patted Dan on the shoulder and said good night.

Dan's aunt helped the family make pallets on the floor in front of the fireplace. Lizzie warmed the quilts by the fire and wrapped the children in them. They were soon asleep. It was only then that Dan told her about the house his uncle had offered them. The news brought Lizzie to tears. It had been a long time since they had known the security of a real home, since they had been able to live without fear of being put out on the street if they couldn't pay the rent. That night she and Dan and the children slept peacefully for the first time in months—and also for the last time for quite a while.

Early the following morning Dan and his uncle

went to Williamston and got gas for Dan's car. They loaded up the little bit of furniture Dan and Lizzie owned and were back in the Islands before noon.

Lizzie and the children were already down at the old house. They had a fire going in the kitchen stove and another in the fireplace in the living room. It seemed to Lizzie that the house was still uncommonly cold, even though she had built the fires before breakfast. But she reasoned to herself that it was an old house, full of cracks and broken windowpanes. She thought that once she plugged the holes her new home would be cozy and safe. Later on she saw it a different way. She remembered that the house hadn't felt safe even in broad daylight that first morning.

When the children heard their father coming down the dirt road honking the car's horn they ran out to meet him. The family had never had much in the way of material possessions, so it wasn't long before the car was unloaded and the few items they owned were in place. By the middle of the afternoon some of their kinfolk had brought them mattresses and a couple of iron bedsteads, which were set up in the one big downstairs bedroom that they all would share.

Lizzie cooked an early supper of dried beans, fatback and cornbread. Then she put the children to bed. It had been a long, hard day, and she and Dan sat down at the kitchen table to enjoy the last of their coffee before they, too, went to bed.

Dan propped his feet on a wooden crate in front of the stove. "I've got me a day's work lined up tomorrow, cutting shingles with some of the men across the swamp," he said to Lizzie. "I reckon I can do that until a regular job comes along. It'll put some meat on the table, at least."

Lizzie heard only part of what Dan was saying, for she had dropped off to sleep without finishing her coffee. Dan finished his cup in silence. His head had just begun to nod when he and Lizzie were brought to their feet by the sound of terrified screams coming from the bedroom.

They ran as quickly as they could. The children were frantically clutching each other, huddled in the middle of their bed. Their sheet, quilts and pillows were scattered all around the room, as if dispersed by a whirlwind. Dan and Lizzie scrambled over the twisted array of bedclothes to try to comfort them.

The children were still incoherent even after Dan and Lizzie carried them into the warm kitchen. Several minutes passed before they were calm enough for their parents to understand them.

"Oh, Papa," the little girl began. "It was a bad man that came after us. He was red and little and he jumped right out of the wall and sat on the foot of the bed and pointed his finger at us. He said he would get us if we didn't leave his house and then he started jumping up and down on Brother. I had to push and push to make him go away and he didn't leave until he heard you and Mama coming. I was so scared." The girl was still sobbing and clutching Dan around the neck.

"He was heavy, too, Papa," the little boy cried. "He jumped up and down on my chest and I pushed and pushed and he wouldn't go away."

"He threw our quilt and sheet on the floor and he kept saying, 'Get out of my house, get out of my house,'" sobbed the little girl.

Dan and Lizzie looked at each other over the children's heads, not knowing what to make of such a tale. They had seen the covers scattered all over the floor, but they were both inclined to treat the whole episode as a nightmare.

They sat in front of the stove rocking and talking softly to the distraught children until the brother and sister finally calmed down and drifted back to sleep. Lizzie gently eased the little boy from her lap and into a chair and then went to the bedroom, where she put the sheet and quilts back on the bed. The more she thought about it the less she believed in the children's Little Red Man. She suspected that one of them had dreamed it and awakened in fright, and that the other one had gotten scared and joined right in. But even though she didn't believe the story she had an uncomfortable feeling while she was in the bedroom. She felt as though someone or something was watching her. Lizzie finally decided that the whole family had a case of nerves from the excitement of getting a house to live in and plenty to eat.

When everything seemed in order she started out of the bedroom to go back to the kitchen. Just then she heard a faint noise from the corner of the bedroom closest to the window. Lizzie stood very still just inside the door and waited. The only light came from the glowing coals of the dying fire in the living-room fireplace, which gave the bedroom walls a weird, reddish cast, while the corners of the room remained dark and menacing. As she stood motionless, allowing herself only half-breaths, she got the distinct feeling that she was not alone in the room.

Then, so quickly that her eyes barely caught the movement, a child-size form raced from the dark corner and right past her, heading through the living room and out the front door. She had seen one thing for certain. The little man—if indeed he happened to be human—was dressed all in red from the cap on his head to the boots on his feet.

Lizzie closed and bolted the front door. When the Little Red Man brushed by her in his hasty exit she had felt a distinct sense of evil emanating from him, and she was afraid for her family. She tried to compose herself as she walked to the kitchen. Dan and the children were asleep, so she gently shook everyone awake. Then they all went together to the bedroom.

The children began to whimper the moment they

entered the room, crying and begging to sleep with their parents. So the family snuggled together in one bed and rested fitfully through the cold night. Lizzie remained more awake than asleep. She thought she felt the sinister presence of the Little Red Man as he slipped back into his dark corner during the murky predawn hours. But the Little Red Man did not bother them again that night.

Dan was up early, but Lizzie already had the kitchen fire built and breakfast cooking when he sat down at the table. Neither mentioned the previous night's strangeness. By six o'clock Dan was ready to leave to cut shingles with the other Islanders.

Lizzie had plenty to keep her occupied. She was soon at work scrubbing and cleaning. When the children got up she fed and dressed them and gave them chores to do. At noon she made sandwiches for the three of them, and only then did she encourage the children to talk about the Little Red Man. They seemed reluctant to discuss their experience, so Lizzie decided that perhaps the sooner it was forgotten the better off they all would be.

It was long past dark when Dan finally got home from his day of cutting cypress shingles. He had hauled a load of shingles into Williamston and been paid cash money for them, and he was the happiest he had been in a long time.

The children had gone to sleep lying on the floor in

front of the stove. Dan and Lizzie carried them to the bedroom and tucked them in their quilt-laden bed. As she left the room Lizzie made sure the bedroom door was left open, so the heat from the fire would keep the children warm.

While Dan ate his supper they talked about the day's work they had done. Neither of them mentioned the Little Red Man, but it was as though he were an invisible barrier between them, and it wasn't long before they ran out of things to talk about. By nine o'clock Dan was ready for bed. He left Lizzie in the kitchen sewing by the light of the kerosene lamp. The children were sound asleep when he crawled into the other bed. He was dog-tired from his hard day's work, and he was asleep almost before his head was on the pillow.

Dan had never been one to awaken easily, but he sensed that someone or something was whispering to him. As he slowly roused he experienced the feeling that a weight was pressing down upon him. When he tried to sit up it felt as though he were being smothered by a hundred-pound bag of cornmeal upon his chest. He summoned all his strength and pushed at the weight. As the palms of his hands made contact with the unseen obstacle, flinging it into the corner of the room, he could feel the hair on the back of his neck stand straight up. His hands had touched something that was living and breathing, but cold as steel.

The scant flame left in the fireplace gave off just enough light for Dan to recognize the creature the children had described the previous night. The Little Red Man was infuriated at having been tossed aside. "Get out of my house!" he screamed. "Get out of my house or you'll be sorry! I'll make you sorry you were ever born!" He scampered out of the corner where Dan had cast him and hurried across the room on his short, red-clad legs, then hopped onto the foot of the bed. "I've run off better men than you," he said. "You'll have no rest as long as you stay under this roof." With that final threat he leaped off the bed and ran out the door and through the house.

By then the children were awake and crying, reliving the terror of the night before. When Lizzie roused and came to the bedroom door she was greeted by turmoil. She understood that the horrid little red creature had invaded her home and terrorized her family again. She also understood that they could not endure another such night of anguish.

Dan was furious and terrified and speechless at what he had just witnessed. At first he wanted to pack up and leave right then, but cold weather and common sense persuaded him to keep his family in the unwelcoming house for the rest of the evening. So they built up the fire in the living room and made a pallet of quilts on the floor, then settled in for the night. It was well into the morning hours before the children finally quit trembling and crying and went to sleep, totally exhausted. Dan and Lizzie lay awake all night fiercely alert, guarding against the evil creature's return. But they were not bothered again that night by the Little Red Man.

It was with mixed feelings that they packed their belongings the following morning. They knew that sleeping was bound to be difficult for some time, wherever they made their home next. Lizzie turned to look back at the house that had given them such inhospitable shelter, and for just a moment she thought she saw the Little Red Man standing on the porch, an evil grin on his flushed face. But when she blinked and looked again the porch was empty.

It is said that people finally gave up trying to live in the old house. It remained empty until time and the elements reduced it to a heap of rotted wood. We can only surmise that the Little Red Man was left to whatever peace his kind may enjoy.

There are some who say that when the house finally disintegrated the Little Red Man disappeared along with it. Others say not, for there is another house on another road not very far away where no one can ever manage to stay for long. But that is another story altogether.

15 | *The Hanging Church*

hurches have always been an important part of the lives of rural people. In remote areas, many of them linked to the outside world by dirt roads, churches were often the center of their communities.

Many country churches had their beginnings in brush arbors, until time and money allowed the construction of small one-room structures for worship services. Few country churches were fortunate enough to have a full-time preacher—that was a luxury that even many town churches were unable to afford. Traveling preachers—circuit riders, as some were known—called on their backwoods charges as often as they could, according to their schedules and the weather. When a real preacher wasn't available a deacon held Sunday school and prayer service. That same deacon was most often in charge of funeral services when the preacher was too far away to make it back for a burial.

Early churches in North Carolina were, by law, part of the Church of England. The Revolutionary War brought the demise of the established church. The nineteenth century then saw churches of all denominations forming in the northeastern part of the state. By far the largest of the religious groups were Baptists and Methodists.

In Washington County, in one of the most remote parts of northeastern North Carolina, there once stood a small clapboard church of indeterminate architecture. Its most appealing feature was the bell tower with a double-door entrance that sat high above the church's rectangular body. The little church was otherwise unremarkable. It was situated back from a dirt road and surrounded by ancient oaks and cedars. It seemed a peaceful enough place, but appearances can sometimes be deceiving.

Churches are universally recognized as places of sanctuary. Church doors traditionally remain unlocked so that those in need of spiritual comfort may find a welcome retreat. Many a distraught soul has entered through those unlocked doors to receive the inner comfort and guidance that earthly sources have denied him. But there are times when even the solace provided by a church will not suffice, times when a man's soul is so tormented that hope is beyond his grasp and reason no longer within his realm of being.

Such must have been the circumstances on a bitterly

cold February night more than a century ago. A light snow had begun to fall in Washington County earlier in the evening, and by midnight the ground was covered deeply enough for passing feet to leave their mark.

A solitary figure, destitute both in soul and body, approached the doors of the tiny clapboard church with the bell tower on top. The pathway to the building was lined with cedars so tall and full that in the fiercely cold wind their branches blew together and entwined, forming an impromptu archway under which the stranger walked. At another time he might have seen the beauty of it, but that night he must have seen only the irony. Head bent into the wind and shoulders slumped in resignation, walking the well-traveled bricks that had for over fifty years led both the joyous and the sorrowful to contemplation and solace, the man felt the snow crunch under his thin shoes as he climbed the steps to the church. A narrow sliver of moonlight cast a glow on the belfry as he hesitantly turned the cold porcelain doorknob.

Once inside he moved cautiously but purposefully in the direction of the bell tower. His resolve weakened only once, when his eye caught the altar at the front of the church. He hesitated only a moment before ascending to the moonlit tower, where he silently closed the door.

The local milkman discovered a grotesque sight the following morning as he was making his rounds in the predawn hours. The fading moonlight cast its last glow on a figure swinging slowly from a rope in the belfry. The frightened milkman urged his old horse to a gallop and sounded the alarm in the little town.

Excitement was rare in that rural community, so when word spread of the hanging at the church the people gathered quickly. When the undertaker and the sheriff finally arrived they had to push their way through a crowd to get to the door. They removed the body from the tiny room. It offered no identification and no clue as to who the poor stranger was, or to why he had ended his life in such a way.

In those days the bodies of the dead were customarily kept in a family parlor until it was time for the funeral. But no one came forward to claim kinship with the stranger, so the pine box holding his remains was placed in the sanctuary of the church. There it rested on rough-hewn sawhorses, sheltered by the altar and the cross.

The community was curious but not heartless. Close by the church was a cemetery, and it was there that the citizens buried the man they had come to know only in death. A simple wooden cross bearing the words "I Came as a Stranger" marked the grave for many years. The passage of time saw the cross decay, until at last there was nothing to identify the grave. People ceased to mention the stranger who had hanged himself in their church.

But the story did not end there. Some years later there was another hanging in the same room of the same church, again a stranger and again a man. The compassionate community buried the victim in the little cemetery beside the first stranger. After that the belfry was padlocked and remained unused.

It wasn't long before the ill-fated church became known as "the Hanging Church." Rumors began to spread that on the first night of a full moon a body could be seen hanging from the bell rope. It did not appear with every full moon, but when it did the reports were always the same. The body was clearly that of a man, and it would swing slowly from side to side for a few minutes before it simply vanished. A few brave souls ventured close enough to report that there was an overturned chair near the rope, but upon closer investigation there proved to be no sign of entry to the room. The door was always securely locked and the windows sealed.

In the early 1900s the clapboard church was torn down to make way for a larger brick structure. The new church, by consent of the entire congregation, was without a belfry. But the vestibule of the new building was erected on the exact spot where the old bell tower had stood. No further reports were heard of a man hanging from a rope, but some older members of the church said they still felt the presence of the dead men. The vestibule had about it a clammy coldness that no amount of heat could temper, whether in winter or even on summer's hottest day. Church members just couldn't seem to enjoy gathering and chatting in the vestibule, and no one lingered anywhere on the premises on nights when the moon was full.

Eventually the brick church burned, and only a mass of rubble was left in its place. For a time so many people came to see the site of the Hanging Church that local residents began to tire of their presence. There is something about the thought of death invading the peacefulness and holiness of a sanctuary that makes people highly uncomfortable, but also morbidly curious.

Today a paved road leads past the site, and most motorists are unaware of the dark history of the old church. The graveyard is still there, overgrown and unkept, marked only by trees and time and the spirits of those who cannot rest on moonlit nights.

16 | *Brotherly Love*

tanding at the end of a winding lane just off the old Red Hill Road outside Plymouth were the sagging remains of a farmhouse. Rot and mildew had assaulted the upstairs windows, leaving them as dark and black-ringed as the eyes of the raccoons that rambled freely about the yard. The one remaining shutter, dove-gray with age and decay, hung by a single rusty hinge, every gust of wind bringing it closer to its demise. A pile of crumbling bricks was all that remained of what had once been a chimney. The gaping hole in the side of the house only added to its grotesque appearance.

The house had been empty for many years, but it stood expectant and watchful, as though waiting for something to happen. No one came there anymore—no one living, that is. More than one passerby related hearing eerie sounds coming from inside the house, and there were a multitude of tales of a headless apparition that carried a lit oil lamp from room to room. No one wanted to be caught near the old homeplace after dark, for there were too many unanswered questions about the two violent deaths that had occurred there.

At their best July and August are torrid, sweltering months in northeastern North Carolina. The morning sun seems to rise from the lush green grass to enfold humanity in an inescapable bubble of dripping heat. Short tempers, old grievances and borderline insanity feed on the steamy heat, and sometimes the intolerable becomes the unbearable and the thin thread of endurance snaps—with a gunshot.

So it must have been on a couple of excruciatingly hot days in July 1954. Will, Buck and Junior were bachelor brothers. They lived in the rambling old two-story house where they had grown up. Trouble had been brewing between Buck and Junior for a long time, but matters were just then coming to a head.

Buck had two guns that he highly prized—a rifle and a double-barreled shotgun. He took good care of them, keeping them under lock and key in his room. One Monday he put his wide-brimmed straw hat on his head and walked the four miles to town. He went early in the morning and was waiting when the hardware store opened up. He purchased two boxes of gun shells and returned home at midday. No one knew it but he was nearly at the breaking point.

Junior was the youngest of eight brothers and a

sister. He was only an infant when his father drowned in the frigid December waters of the Roanoke River. He became the pet of the family after that. His older siblings pampered him and indulged his whims as though only he of the nine children had lost a father. Muv, as the children called their fragile and much-adored mother, encouraged the protective attitude of her older children toward their baby brother. By the time Junior was a toddler it was an acknowledged fact that he was Muv's darling boy and could do no wrong.

Junior was still quite young when Buck went to work on the Norfolk and Southern Railroad. Buck was a serious, quiet, hard-working young man. He was diligent in whatever he pursued, and he had never had problems getting or keeping jobs. Farm labor and odd jobs had always put enough change in his pocket to help out at home and keep him clothed in the dapper suits he was partial to wearing. He was in his early twenties when he was offered a job with the rapidly expanding railroad, and he welcomed it as a chance to make good money. He also welcomed it as a release from a home environment crowded with adolescents and itinerant cousins.

Buck had good reason for wanting to get out of the two-story farmhouse. He was unlike his brothers and his sister in the fact that he had never catered to Junior. In fact Buck avoided him as much as possible. Everyone knew that Buck was not particularly fond of children, but it seemed to the rest of the family that he harbored a special dislike for Junior.

Children are uncanny detectors of friends and foes, and Junior was aware early on that his older brother Buck was not his friend. Buck never took him for rides on the old white mule or played hide-and-seek in the stables with him. Even though Buck always had change in his pocket he never offered Junior a nickel for guessing the answer to a silly question, nor did he bring him bags of sweets from his trips to town, as the other brothers did.

Junior knew that he had the rest of the family wrapped around his finger, but Buck was one he just couldn't figure out. Try as he might he could not please his somber elder brother, and as the years rolled by his attempts at pleasantries toward Buck turned to perversities. After a while it was more fun to antagonize Buck than to patronize him, and it was easier, too, for Junior had a devious mind.

The sister was the first to marry, and then one by one the boys married and moved to their own homes. Finally there were only the three brothers—Will, Buck and Junior—left at the homeplace with Muv. Junior, long since grown, never settled down to anything. Will kept a steady job, and when he wasn't working he was either courting or playing cards with some of his buddies. Buck retired from the railroad and drew a small pension. That pension, along with the meager amount Muv got for the farm crops, kept food on the table and paid the taxes.

Junior was downright lazy when it came to keeping a job. The family was respected by the townspeople, so all the local merchants tried to give Junior jobs for the sake of Muv and his brothers. Junior would work a few days or a few weeks, depending upon the patience of the employer, before he either got fired or quit of his own accord.

Junior had another weakness besides the fact that he was not endowed with a work ethic. It was politely referred to as "a little drinking problem" by Muv. Buck put it in a harsher perspective when he stated that Junior was a sot.

Saturday nights were especially bad times. Junior would drink himself into oblivion and more often than not get locked up by the sheriff. It became a ritual on Sunday morning for Buck or Will to go down to the courthouse and bail Junior out of jail and take him home to Muv, who blamed it all on the crowd he ran with.

Then the blow fell. Muv died in her sleep. She had been the force that held the brothers together, and the family began to splinter after her loss. Perhaps out of respect for her the boys had overlooked each other's faults. But now their petty grievances grew into open hostilities, especially between Buck and Junior.

To make matters worse Buck had skin cancer on his

face, and it began to spread. He went from one doctor to another in an effort to find some treatment to keep the disease from worsening, but nothing seemed to work. As the cancer began to eat away at his nose he was in constant pain, and he grew extremely self-conscious about his grotesque appearance.

Junior, aware of his older brother's agony, saw this as one more opportunity to antagonize him. As Buck's face became increasingly red and raw with the ravages of cancer Junior began to refer to him as "Old Meat-head." When he passed Buck in the back hall of the house Junior would hold his nose to indicate that his brother had a malodorous air about him. At every opportunity he would belittle Buck and make fun of him, especially if someone outside the family was around.

On more than one occasion Will had to come be-tween them to prevent a fight after Junior had pushed Buck to the limit with his relentless persecution. One night after a particularly violent disagreement Will heard Buck say to Junior, "That's all right, you good-for-nothing piece of dog meat. Will won't always be here to save your hide. I'll get you when you least expect it." Buck usually meant what he said, and Will took him seriously. But Junior just laughed and made one of his snide remarks.

On that fateful Monday in July 1954, after he had bought his two boxes of gun shells and returned home, Buck spent the remainder of the sweltering day closeted in his downstairs bedroom.

Junior had one of his late mornings. When he finally stumbled from his bedroom and out to the kitchen, where his lunch was usually waiting, he found an empty table. He searched around in the ice chest on the porch and found some ham and cold biscuits, which he proceeded to make into a sandwich of sorts. He wasn't accustomed to having to fix his own lunch, and he didn't like it one bit. He deliberately left the table a mess and went to find Buck, intending to antagonize him with some form of devilment. But after a thorough search of the yard and barns he could not find his older brother. He beat and kicked at Buck's bedroom door but received no reply. Junior finally decided that his brother must have gone out on some prolonged errand, so he crawled back in bed and slept the rest of the hot afternoon away.

Sometime after five o'clock Buck slipped out of his bedroom and went to the kitchen to prepare supper. The heat from the cookstove made the room almost unbearable, but he fried fatback and made bread and boiled some cabbage. When Will got home he and Buck took their plates out on the porch, where it was a little bit cooler, and ate their supper. Junior didn't show up for supper that night.

Bachelors' habits of many years do not vary. Buck and Will sat on the porch until the mosquitoes started biting, and then Will took an oil lamp from the kitchen and lit it and he and Buck sat in the living room and read until bedtime. Will had no way of knowing that when he said good night to his brother it was the last time he would see him alive.

Junior's bedroom was at the front of the house, with a window that opened onto the front porch. That window had at times provided a means of escape when Buck was angry enough to lock Junior in his room. That night, unseen by his brothers, Junior slipped out through his bedroom window and headed for a honky-tonk on the edge of town. It was after four in the morning when one of his pals dropped him off at the end of the lane. Junior had been drinking, and he stumbled up the lane before he finally made it to the front porch, where he dragged himself back through the open window to his room.

Tuesday began as usual. Will left the house early to go down to the Mayflower Cafe for his breakfast of cheese toast and coffee. Buck, always the earliest riser, a habit he retained from his days with the railroad, had been up since dawn. He made his bed and ate his breakfast of fried eggs, bread and coffee, leaving his dishes on the oilcloth-covered table in the kitchen. He then did most of his day's work, which consisted of feeding the few head of livestock left on the run-down farm and picking up the eggs. There was no evidence of lunch having been prepared, which later helped authorities to determine that the events of that day took place between breakfast and lunch.

Next Buck picked up his loaded rifle and walked to Junior's bedroom. The room, even with its window open, reeked of liquor and stale cigarettes. Junior was lying on his back, mouth open and snoring. Buck pressed the barrel of the rifle to Junior's chest. He pulled the trigger and shot his baby brother through the heart.

After leaving Junior's room he propped the rifle in the hallway by the door and went to the stairs in the back hall, where he had left his shotgun resting against a chair. First he untied the laces of his right shoe and removed his shoe and sock. Buck rested the shotgun on the third stair from the bottom and placed the barrel of the gun under his chin. Then he hooked his toe in front of the trigger and pushed with all of his two hundred pounds. The explosion was heard by neighbors on the adjoining farm, who figured that Buck was merely shooting at the crows that plagued the summer corn crop.

Will came in the back door at five o'clock that afternoon. He was shocked to discover the remains of his brother Buck in the blood-covered hall. It was only after Will returned with help that Junior was found dead in his bed.

The pain and disfigurement of cancer had made life intolerable for Buck. That coupled with Junior's constant harassment and aggravating habits may have been what sent him over the edge and caused him to resort to the final desperation of murder and suicide. No one will ever know for sure.

Will was unable to stay in the house where the terrible deaths had occurred. He moved away, and the old homeplace was closed up. Soon there came reports from passersby that something odd was going on inside. It seemed that a headless figure sometimes moved about in the downstairs part of the house at night. The figure would hold a lit oil lamp and place it on a table in the living room and sit in an old wooden rocker and rock back and forth. That rocker was the one that Buck had always sat in.

There were rumors of moans and screams coming from the back hallway of the house. Some teenagers who broke into the house on a dare left in total terror when they saw the headless figure with the lamp and heard the moans. The house soon earned a reputation for being haunted.

The old homeplace fell into ruin after years of neglect. It and the farmland were sold to a developer, and new homes now stand on the former site of the ill-fated farmhouse. It is quiet and peaceful there, as it should be. Let us hope that Buck and Junior have made their peace, too, wherever they are.

17 | *Dymond City, Ghost Town of Martin County*

ost motorists traveling down N.C. 171 between Jamesville and Old Ford are unaware that they are within a short drive of a real, sure-enough ghost town. If, during the daytime, they should turn just past the old Farm Life School and head in the direction of Dymond City they might not see anything to verify the existence of the town except a road sign. But should they take the same route at night it just might be a different story, for it is said that Dymond City by day cannot rival Dymond City by night.

Older residents who live nearby tell stories about the lights that can be seen in Dymond City on dark and moonless nights. Visitors who stop their cars and get out where the old community once stood might hear a train whistle in the distance, or perhaps even voices or a peal of laughter. No one knows why Dymond City has retained a ghostly presence when so many other small communities have passed from existence without a trace. Maybe some background information on the town will be of use to those who would like to try their hand at unraveling the mystery.

It has been over a hundred years since Dymond City was a living, working town. The town was never actually chartered, but it was considered quite a busy community nonetheless. At one time it had over a hundred residents. In Dymond City's earliest days it was predicted that it would become the most prosperous town in Martin County. It was even referred to by visitors as being rather cosmopolitan.

In the beginning Dymond City was called Waring in honor of Philadelphia native Richard Waring, the president of the railroad that created the town. In later years the name was changed to Dymond City to honor a deceased stockholder of the railroad.

That is one story about the naming of Dymond City, at any rate. There is another story that is not quite so pleasant. It seems that the area's undisturbed forestland was the home of that most vile and feared of serpents, the diamondback rattler. Being naturally bad-tempered and contrary the rattlers didn't take too kindly to having their territory invaded by humans. One tale has it that the deadly diamondbacks bit and fatally wounded a number of early woodsmen. Stories were told of the gigantic size of the snakes, some of which were reported to be eight to ten feet in length and as big around as a good-sized young tree. When they stretched out in the dense undergrowth they were sometimes mistaken for logs. Such stories as these gave rise to the tale that Dymond City was named for the rattler. Even though the history books record the spelling as *Dymond* the road sign that directs travelers to the ghost town uses the spelling *Diamond*.

The town came about when a group of Pennsylvania businessmen purchased forty thousand acres of virgin forest in Martin County in 1868. Their firm was chartered as the Jamesville and Washington Railroad and Lumber Company. Francis Lightfoot, a civil engineer from Pennsylvania, came to Jamesville to do the surveying for a railroad route. One local story concerns a six-mile stretch between Jamesville and the community of Deep Run that Lightfoot chose to survey at night. He took his sighting with his transit aimed at a light held by a man in a tall pine tree. For as long as that pine tree stood it was known as the "Six-Mile Pine."

Most of the residents of the rural area were glad to welcome the railroad and its accompanying lumbermill. But there were among them a few people who opposed progress. The Civil War was still fresh on the minds of some residents. The little town of Jamesville, for example, had been devastated during the war—in December 1862 the Union army burned all but three of the town's houses. So even though the railroad represented jobs and a modest prosperity the fact was that it was owned by Yankees, and that didn't appeal to some folks. There were those who still looked upon anyone from the North as an enemy and treated them as such.

The first wreck on the railroad occurred on January 30, 1871, when some of the disgruntled members of the community sabotaged the tracks by placing obstructions on them. Several passengers were seriously injured, and railroad cars were damaged. But the accident slowed down the J & W only temporarily, for the railroad had come to mean money, more money than most local people had ever seen before. The majority of the citizens wanted it to stay.

Probably the best-known and most colorful character who lived in Dymond City was Abraham Fisher, the man hired around 1872 to complete the last thirteen miles of track through the swampland to the town of Washington, North Carolina. Fisher was well-known for his honesty and integrity. He once walked the fourteen miles from his home to Williamston to deliver a document to his lawyer. Upon arriving he reached into his coat pocket to retrieve the paper, only to discover that it wasn't there. Without a pause he said, "I'll step right back home and fetch it."

By the beginning of December 1887 the entire twenty-one miles of track from the Roanoke River in

Jamesville to the Pamlico River in Washington were in operation. The J & W ran three locomotives, two passenger cars, a baggage car and twenty-one freight cars. Timber cut from the vast swampland acreage was easily moved by rail to either port and shipped north by boat. In addition to hauling timber the railroad carried the mail and transported farm products.

Passenger service on the railroad was quite popular. The J & W was affectionately known as "the old Jolt and Wiggle" because the narrow, uneven track provided quite a bumpy ride through the swamps. First- and second-class passengers rode in the same car, the difference being that second-class passengers had to suffer the indignity of jumping out to help gather wood when the train slowed down for refueling.

Dymond City thrived. It had a hotel. The railroad's company store was an imposing structure that housed a post office and general store on the first floor and the postmaster's living quarters on the second floor, not to mention a Sunday-school room on the third floor. For a brief time Dymond City even boasted a school. The enrollment totaled twenty-one students in 1885, with operations overseen by a three-member school board. Dymond City was a typical company town during the late 1880s. The stores and most of the homes were owned by the railroad. Employees lived in company houses and shopped at the company store.

When they needed to travel they rode the company train.

Dymond City's heyday lasted for a quarter of a century, and then one by one the families began to move away for one reason or another. Finally there were so few families left in the town that the post office was closed and mail for the dying community was sent to Griffin's Township.

In April 1927 a fire swept through the ghost town and destroyed the old hotel and all the other buildings, thus erasing the last signs of the town that was once considered Martin County's most promising settlement. Eventually the land was sold to other lumber companies. The streets of the town became overgrown with trees and bushes, and Dymond City gradually went back to wilderness.

But the little town would not let itself be forgotten, not completely. People began to talk of seeing a light that bobbed along where the old tracks once ran. It was most often described as a lantern held in someone's hand—an unseen hand that guided the light as it bounced along.

Others claimed to have seen a ball of fire that rolled along just above the treetops and then suddenly disappeared. There was speculation that it might be the ghost of one of the old railroad men. Some thought it was the spirit of Francis Lightfoot, the railroad's original surveyor, who was known to have used a torch for nighttime surveying.

There are few clues as to why the town should retain an active presence so long after it passed from existence. No one has ever solved the riddle of the Dymond City Lights, but people say they are still there, bobbing and bouncing along where the tracks of the old J & W were laid over a hundred years ago.

If you should ever find yourself in Martin County at night you just might want to take a detour and go down the narrow dirt road that leads to what was once Dymond City. Then you, too, can try your hand at solving the riddle of the old ghost town.

18 | *Aunt Liza and the Sweet Baby Jesus*

unt Liza Goodwin had lived in her little run-down cabin by Lake Phelps for longer than anyone could remember. She claimed to be the oldest person in all of Washington County, and no one dared to dispute her claim.

She was a living contradiction. As far as anyone knew she was no blood kin to a soul, living or dead. She never brought up the subject of kinfolk, but whenever someone asked her about her relatives she would joke in her scratchy old voice, "Ain't got none, and don't want none. Relations is a pestilence. I was hatched by a buzzard and raised up by an old bobcat, so you better not cross me." And with that she'd throw back her bony head and laugh.

Folks said that Aunt Liza wasn't as big as a half-grown youngun but worked like a full-grown man. Her only income came from her patch of tobacco. As soon as the ground thawed she'd hitch old Billy Bob, her white mule, to the plow, and they'd start breaking the ground. People walking by could hear her talking to Billy Bob just like he was a person. "Get along there, you stubborn old cuss," she'd say. "You quit being so ornery or you ain't going to get a mouthful of supper." When folks heard Aunt Liza fussing at Billy Bob they just laughed, for everyone knew that Billy Bob was the laziest mule in the county, and that was because Aunt Liza had made a pet out of him.

Whenever someone was sick or a woman was about to give birth the local residents sent for Aunt Liza. Most of the lake people had never been to a real doctor and probably wouldn't have gone even if they had a chance, for they didn't trust strangers.

Aunt Liza had a basket she'd wove from the tall, strong reeds that grew in the shallows of the lake. Packed inside were tonics, cough syrup, salves, poultices and packets of herbal tea. The sight of her striding by with her medicine basket strapped on her back was a sure sign that somebody needed help. Aunt Liza had a cure for whatever ailed a person. Behind her cabin was a garden where she raised healing herbs. And if she couldn't get patients well with her roots and herbs then she'd just talk the sickness out of them.

When Aunt Liza was called to a birthing she would take care of the whole family, cooking enough food to last until the mother was up and about again. She always made the same gift for every baby she helped into the world—a christening gown. After supper was cooked she'd pull a rocking chair up by the fireplace and get out her sewing bag. Then she'd commence working on the gown. She used the most delicate material imaginable, which she wove herself.

The older children would gather around, and Aunt Liza would tell them stories while she worked. "I do love to make a christening gown for a newborn baby," she'd say. "I reckon you younguns know that when the sweet baby Jesus was born He didn't have nothing but an old rough cloth wrapped around Him. Don't you know if Aunt Liza had been there she would have wove Him up the finest piece of cloth, so soft He would have thought it was angel's hair. Younguns, I sure wish I could have made that baby Jesus a christening robe."

The years went by. Babies that Aunt Liza had helped to birth grew up and left the lake, coming back only for short visits. But on those visits many of them found the time to stop by Aunt Liza's cabin. They never went away empty-handed, as Aunt Liza always had a bag of potpourri or a jar of healing salve or a pint of grape preserves for them to take as a memento of where they were born.

Time didn't seem to slow Aunt Liza down. She tended her tobacco and her cotton and her herbs, planting by the signs of the moon. People fishing on the banks of the lake could often hear the whir of her spinning wheel and the clackety-clack of her old loom as she wove cotton thread into the fine material she used for her christening gowns.

Aunt Liza loved every season of the year. She always said that God changed the seasons to keep people from getting too set in their ways. In the spring she was the first to start plowing her garden. In the summer and fall she picked grapes and berries for jellies and preserves, and she gathered walnuts and hazelnuts for cakes and pies.

Nobody around the lake bothered to start a garden until they saw Aunt Liza working in hers. Even though the others sowed when she sowed and reaped when she reaped their crops were never quite equal to Aunt Liza's. Once someone overheard Aunt Liza talking to her tomato plants. "Look here," she said. "You're a pure humiliation to me, setting here doing nothing. Here it is the third of July and you ain't got a tomato on you as big as a guinea egg. Old man Buck down the road has got tomatoes as big around as a cantaloupe and as red as the sun ball. If you don't get some spunk about you and get to growing I've a good mind to turn that flock of laying hens loose on you." No one could doubt that with Aunt Liza's encouragement her tomatoes were sure to be bigger and juicier than old man Buck's by the end of the season.

Aunt Liza thought that the baby Jesus was the most precious gift ever given to the world, so it was not surprising that her favorite time of year was Christmas. She often told people that she loved Christmas like a hog loved swill.

She started her Christmas baking the first day of December and didn't quit until Christmas Eve. All of those walnuts she had picked up during the year were put into her special egg-white cookies. Those cookies were so light and sweet that biting into one was just the same as eating sweetened air. Aunt Liza also made fruitcakes by the dozen, mixing them up in her big black wash pot and stirring them with a wooden paddle. Once they were baked she wrapped them in brown paper, then loaded them into an old wooden wheelbarrow and delivered them to everyone on the lake.

One night near Christmas Aunt Liza was enjoying a comfortable night's sleep when she had a splendid dream. In the dream she was standing by the manger. There, as big as life, were Joseph and Mary, all surrounded by donkeys, sheep and goats. Hovering above the manger was a band of angels singing the prettiest music she had ever heard.

But the best part of the dream was seeing the baby Jesus lying in the manger, for on His tiny body was a beautiful white christening dress. As Aunt Liza moved closer to get a better look the baby Jesus smiled up at her and reached out His little hands.

When she got up the next morning Aunt Liza understood that her dream had been a sign. She went right to work cutting and sewing the most exquisite christening dress she had ever made, for this one was intended for the sweetest baby the world has ever known. The stitches were so tiny that they could barely be seen. Aunt Liza labored day and night until her work was finished. Then she spread out her very best Star of Bethlehem quilt on her spare bed and laid the baby Jesus' dress atop the quilt to keep it safe and neat.

Aunt Liza then went back to work baking cakes and pies and cookies, until the little cabin was full of the rich odor of spices and the promise of good things to eat. She chopped down the best cedar tree in her woods and, old as she was, dragged it inside the cabin. She sang in her scratchy voice as she trimmed the tree with tinsel and cranberries and strings of popcorn. On every branch she placed one of her hand-dipped candles, and on the very top she placed a crocheted star.

When all was ready she went up and down the lakeshore inviting all her friends to a very special birthday party for the baby Jesus. By that time the whole community had heard about Aunt Liza's dream, and they knew about the christening dress. Many of them had seen the dress and marveled at its beauty, but not a single soul among them believed that *He* would actually be coming to receive His gift.

The day before Christmas was cold and bitter, with the winds off the lake blowing from the north all day long. That night, as friends and neighbors made their way down the pine-needle path to Aunt Liza's, there was much speculation about the party. Some thought Aunt Liza had grown old and foolish and was obsessed about her christening gowns. Others were concerned that she would be terribly disappointed when the baby Jesus did not attend the festivities.

As they approached the cabin the guests were greeted by the warm light from the candles in every window. Inside the cabin the candles on the Christmas tree twinkled cheerfully, while the tinsel reflected the light from the oil lamps. There was a crackling fire in the big stone fireplace, where a tabby cat and her kittens lay basking in the warmth of the hearth.

Aunt Liza was beaming as she greeted her guests. She hugged and kissed every man, woman and child as if they were family. Some even suggested after the events of that night that there was a glow around her, a radiance not unlike that of a halo.

Aunt Liza didn't believe in doing things halfway. Her guests pulled taffy and bobbed for apples. Somebody brought out a fiddle, and everyone began to square-dance. When the guests were worn out with frolicking it was time to load up their plates with Aunt Liza's good food. Every square inch of space in the little cabin was taken up by the time all the company found a seat and began to eat.

When everyone had taken his fill the fiddler began

to play softly, and before long the sound of Christmas carols was in the air. They had just finished singing "Silent Night" when the clock on the mantel struck midnight. A hush fell over the guests, for above the bed where the christening gown lay there was a light. At first it was only a flicker, but then it grew brighter and brighter until all around the little gown there was a glow. Then came the sweetest singing that earthly ears had ever heard.

No one stirred. The guests hardly dared to breathe, for from the oldest to the youngest they knew that they were witnessing a miracle. When the light faded away the little christening gown was gone and the room was filled with an unearthly stillness. The baby Jesus had received His birthday gift.

Aunt Liza sat in her rocking chair by the fire with her head slumped on her chest, a smile still on her wrinkled old face, her gnarled hands no longer busy, but resting in her lap. She had seen the baby Jesus, and her work was done. She had given the beloved baby His christening gown, the finest present that she had to offer. And the baby Jesus had given her the greatest gift of all, that of eternal peace.

A NOTE ON THE TYPE

The text of this book was set in Galliard, a typeface designed by Robert Granjon in the 16th century. Through computer technology the italic type used for the chapter titles has been extended and tightened to enhance Galliard's elegant yet contemporary style.